THE TOWER, THE MASK,
AND THE GRAVE

THE TOWER THE MASK & THE GRAVE

a mystery novel by

BETTY SMARTT CARTER

Harold Shaw Publishers
Wheaton, Illinois

Author's Note: I made this up. Not one dadgum person place or thing in the whole dadgum book, not even a comb or a fork, has any resemblance to anything I ever saw heard tasted smelled or felt. Honest.

copyright © 1997 by Betty Smartt Carter

ISBN 0-87788-559-1

Cover design by David LaPlaca

Library of Congress Cataloging-in-Publication Data

Carter, Betty Smartt, 1965-
    The tower, the mask, and the grave / Betty Smartt Carter.
      p. cm.
    ISBN 0-87788-559-1(pbk.)
    I. Title.
  PS3553.A7733T68   1997
  813'.54—dc21   96-37643
                                          CIP

---

04 03 02 01 00 99 98 97

10 9 8 7 6 5 4 3 2 1

To Virginia, Lyle, and Marjorie, in memory of our
dear friend and secretary, Evelyn

Emmet College
Campus Map

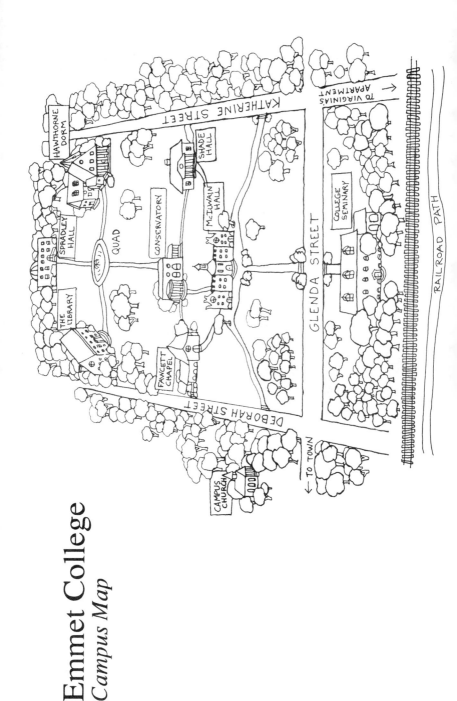

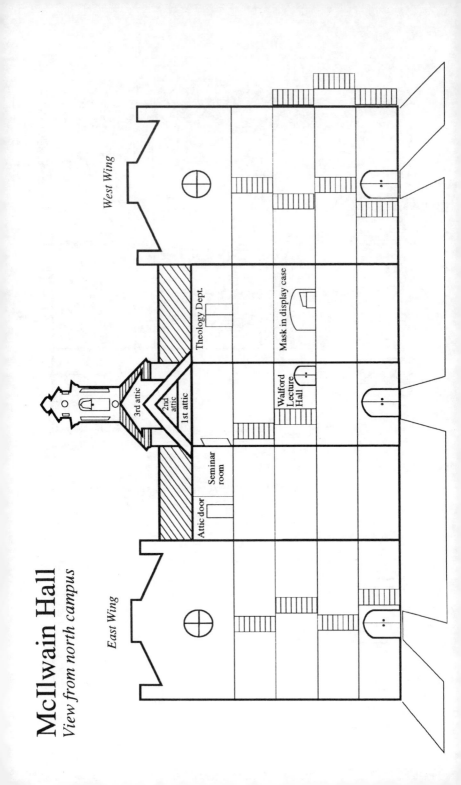

McIlwain Hall
View from north campus

West Wing

East Wing

3rd attic

2nd attic

1st attic

Attic door

Seminar room

Theology Dept.

Walford Lecture Hall

Mask in display case

McIlwain Hall
View from south campus

West Wing

Theology Dept. Offices

Entrance to lower attic

East Wing

A List of Characters

Mark Erlichson   Youngest and hairiest member of the Emmet College theology department.

Virginia Falls   Our heroine. Avoids mistletoe whenever possible but has a passion for the truth.

Stephen Holc   Loves Virginia. Dreams of conducting the London Symphony with a spatula.

Milton Katharde   Wise and respected head of the theology department. He lives with a secret sorrow.

Howard Molliby   Wears bow ties, sneezes a lot, speaks in Latin.

Edward Nimitz   His heart belongs to Lucy Trapp, but he may need a pacemaker.

Lucy Trapp   Weeps freely and fosters fond feelings for Edward Nimitz. But is there something criminal between them?

Florence Treadwell   Gone, but not forgotten.

Raymond Treadwell   Forgotten, but not gone.

1

The Tribe of Intellectuals

AN AFRICAN MASK LAY IN A GLASS case on the third floor of McIlwain Hall. It stared through the dark at nothing in particular, even when a cough rang out and a girl lingered for a moment in the quiet corridor. Christmas break had just swept over Emmet College, scattering students like dead leaves, bringing a snow as pure as the freshman class to the wide campus lawns. Virginia Falls hadn't met a living soul on her way to work—not on the street, not at the railroad crossing, not on the icy sidewalk that snaked up the front lawn of the college. Usually, just as she stepped off the wooded path that raced the train tracks across the entire state of Illinois, Florence Treadwell pulled by in an old blue Nova, stuck her head out the window like a golden retriever, and said, "Why won't you ride with me, Virginia? This car is too big for one person."

"Florence, I refuse to ride three blocks to work. You ought to get out and walk."

"I'm too old, dear. See you in the office!"

But this morning, Virginia hadn't met anyone. She stood alone now in the dark building, listening. She heard no footsteps, no creak of floorboards upstairs, no distant flush of toilets. No breeze rippled down from doors opened and shut out of sight, on other floors. And yet she knew that upstairs, above this peaceful place, Dr. Katharde already sat at his great octagonal table, spinning out long sentences, knitting them together with semicolons, decorating them with exclamation points. Just the thought of him up there made her feel crushed down, like a spring in a mattress.

She left the mask, which she stopped to look at nearly every day, and climbed the central stairs. Two flights brought her to a fifth-floor hallway, so cold that she could see her breath. Halfway down the hall, on the right, sat the Department of Theology. She hesitated, then put her hand on the knob. Locked.

"He has to be here," she said softly. Her voice broke the amazed quiet. She unlocked the office and stepped inside, staring at his closed door, at the stained-glass roses that hovered on the transom. She waited for a light to flicker on, for the roses to glitter like jewels, for a cough or a sigh on the other side of that door. When nothing came, she sat down at her desk, without taking off her coat or hat. His manuscript awaited her, as usual, with a yellow note attached:

(Thursday, 9:30 P.M.) To Miss Falls: I shall arrive late in the day tomorrow. Do not despair! You shall be kept to the grindstone! Read chapter 10 and give me your comments by this afternoon. She who hesitates is lost!

Virginia closed her eyes. So he would arrive late. She leaned over and put her forehead to the manuscript. In the distance, the clock on the chapel steeple chimed once. 7:30, Friday morning, December 16. Last day of work, nine days left till Christmas. She lifted her head, slipped a red pencil between her teeth, and gathered strength to look once again at the mound of white paper.

Christ on Trial: A Defense of God
by
Milton P. Katharde

She sliced the manuscript in half and pulled out a chunk as thick as a slice of French bread.

"Chapter 10: 'Why Do the Wicked Prosper?'" He'd rewritten this chapter how many times now? nineteen? twenty? The same went for all the other chapters, not to mention the introduction and postscript. Dr. Katharde had high hopes for this book; he intended it to be his magnum opus, his final defense of Christianity, and a bold summation of his thought. He had passed his seventieth birthday, after all. Forty years ago, *Time* magazine had placed him on its cover, over the headline "God vs. Satan, K-O in the 1st Round." That article hung, yellow and brittle, in a frame above Florence's desk. It announced a bright new renaissance among American evangelicals, all heralded by the brilliant young Katharde's surprise bestseller *How to Argue with the Devil.* "Milton Katharde," the article said, "intends to be an American C. S. Lewis, an apostle to doubters, a missionary to the tribe of intellectuals."

Virginia had heard the line about the tribe so many times that she wanted to scream. It reminded her of everything else at Emmet College, oozing with missionary zeal. At what other three-and-a-half-star institution of higher learning could you buy mosquito netting in the campus bookstore? At what other top-100 liberal arts college could you watch a basketball game in the Hall of Martyrs? Dr. Katharde had the look of a suffering martyr. Even when he smiled, you expected him to pitch over in your arms, arrow shafts sticking out of his back.

"Miss Falls," he'd announced when he hired her shortly after her graduation, "I invite you to assist me in my mission to the formidable tribe of intellectuals."

"Well," she'd said, "I just hope they're not cannibals."

Most of a year had gone by. She'd poured over a thousand pages of his argument for the existence of God. She'd scratched out his exclamation points and unraveled his sentences, tying up dangling participles like loose wires. But she didn't believe his arguments, and she didn't like his book, and she certainly didn't worship Dr. Katharde the way Florence Treadwell did. "Such a man," Florence would say, "a great man. Every word he speaks a pearl of wisdom."

In a certain way, Virginia still wished she could agree. She had a religious streak in her, people had always said so, and there had been a time when she'd thought of becoming a missionary herself. As a teenager she had escaped home (sweet rebellion) by passing more than a little bit of time at a north Florida United Methodist church, singing in the choir, soberly scribbling notes while the elderly minister rambled on about Albert Schweitzer and *Jonathan Livingston Seagull.*

And then a family of musical Baptists—the Singing Nordquists—visited her church, genuine heart-changed, born-again Christians from the Midwest. The Reverend Nordquist boomed out "Just As I Am" from the altar, and she walked the aisle. Later, in the choir room behind the sanctuary, he pointed her to Illinois for college. "Go to Emmet," he said. "It's a good place for a young lady who wants to serve the Lord.

17

It'll help you find God's will for your life, not to mention a Christian husband." It sounded so good, going a thousand miles from home. She ordered a college sweat shirt and worked three summers at a dairy farm just to pay for her freshman year. Once at Emmet, she wound up taking Dr. Katharde's freshman Bible class. His authority was stunning, a clap of thunder in her calm sky. She went home the summer of her freshman year announcing that she planned on going into full-time Christian service. Her father laughed. "Ginny don't smoke and she don't chew," he'd said with a sneer, "going to marry a preacher and the devil with you."

"I just hope God sends me a million miles from Florida," she had growled back at him. "I'd rather spend my entire life in Africa than stay one day longer in the same house with an atheist!"

She'd traded her family for Christianity, higher learning, and the broad Illinois sky. Just too bad that religion had turned out to be a seasonal thing, an Easter lily, springing up when she was a lonely adolescent and now more or less dead. How it had finally died was a story she hadn't yet told anyone, but anyway, it was dead, and she no longer belonged at Emmet. In dreams, sometimes, she saw herself standing on an empty plain, blown here and there, a weed in the wind, belonging neither to this place nor any other. And then, waking up, she thought of home and her mother, and she longed to go back. But she could live with the longing. She couldn't live with her father again, not even for a day.

Outside, long blue shadows stretched over the perfect white. The office door opened and shut. Virginia didn't turn around.

"Morning, dear," said Florence Treadwell. She had a high, clear voice and hair as white as the light in the windows. Sometimes it made you squint.

"Good morning," said Virginia. "I was worried when I didn't see you drive by."

"Well, I was worried when I didn't see you on the road. Guess you're getting an early start." Florence looked at Dr. Katharde's closed door, and her small mouth fell open. "Where is he?"

"He left me a note. He'll be in late."

Florence hesitated for a moment, then nodded. "Oh, yes, yes, yes, that's right. He has a meeting this morning. Virginia, you still have your coat on."

"Yes, ma'am."

"You're all flushed." Florence's voice rose even higher. She came across the room as Virginia unzipped her jacket. "You're not sick, are you? Do you have a fever?"

"I'm always flushed."

"You know, don't you, that red, flushed skin is a sign of hypochondria."

"Hypothermia."

"Exactly. That's what I meant." Florence pushed back Virginia's dark curls and laid a petite hand on her forehead.

"There's nothing wrong with me," Virginia said a little weakly.

"I think that Florida sunshine will do you some good this Christmas."

"I'm not going home for Christmas."

"What?"

"I'm staying here. I need the peace and quiet."

Florence sat down in front of Virginia and stared. "How old are you, my dear?"

"Twenty-three."

"A twenty-three-year-old needs peace and quiet? No, an old lady like me needs peace and quiet, and I have five grandchildren coming. What you need is family. You go home for Christmas."

The department door opened just then, and Dr. Erlichson came in. He was the youngest and hairiest of the professors, with a long tangle of dark beard that usually had crumbs in it. Several times a day he loped over from his office across the hall to look for leftover food in the department refrigerator.

"Hungry again?" said Virginia as he passed by her desk, heading for the Frigidaire.

"My wife doesn't cook breakfast," he said. "She says she's not my slave, she's a professional in her own right."

"And I don't suppose you could make your own breakfast?"

"I think Dr. Molliby might have left something in here. Aaach! Rancid tuna!"

"What will you be doing for Christmas, Mark?" asked Florence. "Visiting family?"

"I'm afraid so," he said as he stuffed a jelly doughnut into his mouth. "You know how it is at Christmas with your family. You drop thirty years, suddenly you're arguing with these other adults about why somebody sat in your chair when you went to the refrigerator."

"Poor Mark, that must come up so often—"

"Why travel?" asked Virginia. "Stay here."

"This Christmas I have no choice. My Uncle Myron's in the hospital."

"Myron? Oh dear," Florence said, looking suddenly concerned. "What's wrong with Myron?"

"Just an accident. Nothing to worry about."

"I take it you know Dr. Erlichson's uncle," said Virginia.

Florence smiled widely. "I used to know him very well. He was a student in the department. *So* charming!" She batted her eyelashes. "And a practical joker, too. One time he threaded fishing line through the chapel ceiling right down to the podium. Milton gave the opening prayer, and by the time he was finished, the Bible had been snatched up to heaven."

"Surely Dr. Katharde *noticed* the fishing line," said Virginia.

"Of course he did," said Florence, "but he didn't want to spoil a good prank. You see? People say Milton doesn't have a sense of humor, but he does."

Dr. Erlichson coughed loudly.

"You know, Mark," said Florence, "you and your wife ought to invite Virginia to go along with you to Michigan. Virginia will be by herself this Christmas."

"By herself?" said Dr. Erlichson. "Don't you have a boyfriend, Virginia? Isn't there that guy—that what's his name, the pianist who used to go here?"

"He's just a friend," Virginia said.

"Oh yeah? I've seen you and that guy. That guy worships you. He's just melting, just oozing all over the place when you're in the room."

"Hush."

Florence was typing, picking up great speed. Dr. Erlichson tapped the side of her typewriter. "Has Milton put another atheist in your hands?"

"I'm writing to R.F., poor soul," said Florence, her head bobbing up and down as her fingers drummed the keyboard. "Retired college professor, currently apostate. Been corresponding with this one for several months now. Oops! I shouldn't talk and type at the same time. Another typo."

"And what are you telling him?"

"I'm quoting Milton. 'You, my friend, are at a point of transition between blind faith and seeing faith. You are so used to believing without seeing that you forget you have eyes to see with at all. Doubt is like a light under the door when you're standing in the dark—it lets you know where you need to go. It reminds you of what you're looking for.'" The bell dinged suddenly on her typewriter, and she started a new line.

"When did MPK say that?" asked Dr. Erlichson.

"Walking on Water, page 13."

"Well, I'll leave the Milton scholarship to you." Dr. Erlichson stood up with a carton of milk in his hand. "Incidentally, I asked Dr. Molliby what he wanted for Christmas, and he gave me the strangest lecture—said there'd be no Christmas celebrations in this office now or ever, and it all had something to do with the great pyramidical structure of the universe. I take it he's opposed to parties."

Florence shook her head but kept typing. "Howard and his pyramids. It's Milton who's against parties, not Dr. Molliby."

"Milton? Oh, I see. Happiness, bah. Fun, humbug."

"That's not it at all. Milton's no Scrooge. He and his wife used to give lovely parties before she died."

"Of course they did." He headed out the door, calling, "Daddy's coming, Tiny Tim!"

Florence sighed. Virginia scribbled on the manuscript: "Dr. K., it's best not to italicize entire paragraphs."

For the rest of the morning, no one else came in, not even frail, sickly Dr. Nimitz, who had the door next to Dr. Katharde's. (Dr. Erlichson called it "death's door.") Later in the day when the afternoon sky glowed pale orange in the window, Virginia put Dr. Katharde's manuscript aside and looked past a geranium at a tall figure moving straight across the lawn far below, hurdling an icy sidewalk and plunging his boots into a drift, lifting his long legs high until he reached the driveway circling McIlwain Hall.

"Dr. Katharde is coming," she said.

Florence came to the window. "Goodness, he is." She went back to her desk and began shuffling through a large file, glancing up at the door every few seconds. Before long, Dr. Katharde came into the office, snow still on his pant legs.

"Last day before vacation," he said wearily and removed his coat and his furry hat. He laid them across Florence's right arm, then he carefully peeled off his gloves and draped them across her left. She swept away into his office. It was like watching a knight with his page.

"Miss Falls," he said. "How is that manuscript coming?"

"I've done what you asked me to do."

"Oh, excellent. Let me have it. Thank you. And what, my dear critic, did you think of this chapter? Did I convince you that God is fair?"

She hesitated. She never knew how much of the truth to tell him. He saw through compliments. *"Truth,* Miss Falls! Truth shall not bend the knee to Baal!"

She sank down in her chair. "Dr. Katharde, I changed some of your wording, and I removed most of your exclamation points."

"You did!"

"Yes, sir."

He put his hand to his forehead and looked

around for Florence, who was just coming back into the room. "Florence, did you finish that letter to the board of the Institute for Intellectual Evangelism? I wanted to look it over."

"I finished all your letters. I stamped them with your signature, sealed them up, and put them in the mail basket," she said. "I didn't know when you'd be coming in. The carbons are on your desk, when you have a chance to look at them."

He looked suddenly worried. "But what will you do if I find a mistake? Will you retype the letter? I don't want any of that messy correction fluid on my correspondence—"

"As I've told you many times before, Milton, I'll simply roll the letter back on the platen, match the crosses on my *t*s with the red cross on the plastic marker, and then make my correction. See? Who needs a computer when they have red crosses on their plastic marker? Now have a cup of coffee and warm up."

"Thank you, but I shall get straight to work. And, Miss Falls, I'll take this manuscript into my office and peruse it." He headed toward his office, and Virginia thought of following him. What if she told him? What if she told him about her disbelief, beginning with the whole dysfunctional family/Albert Schweitzer bit? She looked down and pretended to be busy, but for a strange moment her confession hung beneath her, urging her on, a cliff without a guardrail—jump, jump.

"Not much of the afternoon left," said Florence, getting back to her typing. "And I'm supposed to leave early. My daughters are flying in this evening. Oh dear! I forgot to put my carbon in. Where is my mind?"

"Just make a photocopy," said Virginia.

"You know I don't comprehend that machine, Virginia. When the world runs out of carbon paper, that's when I'll make photocopies, not before. Look at this—I have to type the whole letter over, and I'm practically out of correction ribbon, too; I've made so many silly mistakes. I guess my mind's on Christmas. Goodness, Virginia, listen to those chapel bells ringing 4:00 already." She stopped to hear the last gong and then began singing along with the chimes as she typed—"Oh come, all ye faithful, hmm hmm hmm hmm hmm hmm—"

Dr. Katharde popped out of his office, suddenly. "Florence, help me. I've spent the last fifteen minutes trying to talk my way out of the Christmas pageant at Fawcett Chapel. They've drafted Dr. Nimitz too. Poor old Edward, he'll have to wear those horn-rims of his under his wise man's turban. Oh, the humiliation! Can't you think of anything I have to do on Wednesday night?"

"Why don't you try to get into the spirit of it?" said Florence. "It brings joy to so many people."

Dr. Katharde sighed. *"Et tu, Florence? Et tu?"*

She smiled as his door closed again. The

afternoon came quickly to an end, but Virginia kept all these things and pondered them in her heart.

2

Confounding the Enemy

"EMMET COLLEGE," VOWED ITS FOUNDER, Herbert McIlwain, "shall promote liberty without liberalism. It shall serve as a fortress of freedom, standing strong against the forces of slavery and oppression."

McIlwain was a preacher, an evangelist, a fierce abolitionist who stormed the South, calling down fire and brimstone on slave owners. Not a theologian by training, he still had the sense to see that preaching alone couldn't shore up religion and hold back slavery in the territories. He canvassed the prairie, convincing the Christian people of the Middle West to help him found a college that would educate whites and blacks in the same manner, on the same premises.

What freedom needed, he said, was higher education. Professors. Books. Diplomas. With donations from churches, he purchased land in Emmet, Illinois, and built McIlwain Tower on the property's highest point. With limestone from nearby Joliet, he piled the blocks twenty feet, fifty feet, eighty feet high to touch the broad sky. "Do not think, brothers," he said at the dedication, "that I am erecting a Tower of Babel, a tower of human learning and human arrogance. My tower is a humble one, which must erode with time. Only the Word of God stands forever, and the Word of God is an eternal proclamation of freedom."

The Tower finished, he added east and west wings of his own rambling design, cluttered with curling stairways and narrow passageways. "I wish to confound the enemy," he said and garnished the whole building with limestone parapets, so that from the bottom of the hill it did look like a fortress braced for war. A handful of teachers soon wandered in from the south and east, then a score of students, and Herbert McIlwain presided over them all from an office in the attic of the Tower.

Each day he retired to a small wood-frame house fifty yards northwest of the building, site of the future Fawcett Chapel. That happy arrangement lasted for five years. Then a new matter captured his attention—the Civil War. He volunteered himself as a Union army chaplain and headed south with a black regiment called the Liberators. While his college suffered through hard winters and influenza without him, the Liberators rode across the ruins of Georgia. Disease and starvation followed. No one wanted to feed a black regiment in hungry times, not even the Union army. Some men died in raids, but most died of dysentery, including McIlwain. When the word of his death reached Emmet, Illinois, the whole town mourned. Streets and parks took his name. Statues arose in his honor. And not long afterwards, people began to say that slave tunnels carved up the ground under McIlwain Tower. They said that Herbert McIlwain had been a conductor on the Underground Railroad. Over 130 years later, those legends persisted.

When Virginia left McIlwain Hall on this December afternoon, darkness had settled in the knotted passageways—such deep darkness that she imagined herself walking through tunnels now, even three floors up. She didn't bother to visit the mask when she left the central stairwell, turned east, and descended another winding flight of steps. Reaching the first floor, she paused to pull on her mittens and scarf. Then she took the south door to front campus. It was clear out now, not snowing. Christmas trees lit the front lawn. A few car lights flitted back and forth on Glenda Street, in front of the college seminary.

"Hello!" shouted someone far down toward Campus Church—it was Dr. Trapp, wearing a matted fur coat and black beanie. Dr. Trapp wore hats of all kinds: beanies, caps, hoods, and occasionally, at the height of spring, wide, flimsy bonnets. "Look," she said, waddling forward breathlessly in tall boots. "Look at the engraving I bought for Edward." Edward Nimitz was as old as Dr. Katharde, a good twenty years older than Dr. Trapp, but Virginia had noticed the shy, tender looks they exchanged when they sat across from each other at department meetings. Sometimes they sat talking in his office after everyone else had gone home.

"Abelard and Héloïse?" guessed Virginia, examining the print.

"Yes," said Dr. Trapp, with a tiny smile. "Edward pointed it out to me the other day and said he'd always liked it. I think it reminds him of us." She let out a long sniff, perhaps a laugh. "But he never buys anything for himself. So I'm going to surprise him." She put her hand up to her mouth. "I'm a little embarrassed. Is it too much?"

"Too much of what?"

"You know." She lifted her hand higher, to her hat. "Too much between two close friends."

"I don't know." Virginia pictured poor Dr. Nimitz looking at that picture from behind his thick glasses. He might have a stroke if he thought too hard about Abelard and Héloïse.

"Well," said Dr. Trapp, "I'll go up to the

department and show it to Florence. Is she still working?"

"She had to leave early," said Virginia. "But Dr. Katharde's still hard at work."

"Oh my! And I thought wild horses couldn't drag Florence away if Milton had need of her!" She laughed out loud. "So long, Virginia." Virginia walked on, past Campus Church, under bare maples, all the way to town. She went into Rupprecht's Hardware and looked at tools, then wandered to the art-supplies store.

"Can I help you?" asked a skinny boy with a nose ring. She shook her head and went out again, continuing to the bookstore. Stephen, her pianist friend who was always oozing and melting, liked novels about decapitated prom queens and demon-possessed dogs. "Each to his own," he always said, as she picked up John Donne. After five minutes of browsing in Suspense, she left the bookstore behind. She searched for a tie. No luck.

She walked home quickly, taking the route through town and avoiding the wooded path by the train tracks. Even on a snowy night, it was too dark for a woman alone. That's what Stephen said, anyway. "Don't take the railroad path by yourself at night. Remember that book I gave you about the 'eyeball killer.' You need an escort, or at least goggles."

Her apartment sat on top of a large house belonging to some retired missionaries. The Viksmas. "Like the vapor rub," said Mr. Viksma.

On warmer mornings, the Viksmas did graceful, dance-like exercises in the back yard. They'd learned the exercises in Africa, adding just a few elements of their own, such as clasping their hands in prayer during deep knee bends. Virginia wondered if they didn't like Stephen's coming over so much—his bounding loudly up the side steps at all hours and banging on her door. "Virginia! I know you're in there!" Actually, being the son of the college orchestra conductor, Stephen behaved like the very model of a gentleman. He'd only kissed her once. It had happened just a few Saturday mornings ago, after a Friday night argument. He banged on her door in the middle of a cartoon.

"Go away," she said. "I'm watching Daffy Duck."

"But I love you."

"I don't love you, Stephen."

"I'll make you lunch."

"It's only 10:28."

"Brunch, then. Please let me apologize. Let me in."

She opened the door, he knocked her backwards off her feet, and they kissed on the floor for two minutes. The memory of those two minutes still made her feel a little weak, like a heroine in the kind of paperbacks Florence was always reading on her lunch hour. But it hadn't happened again.

Tonight, she stood at the foot of the steps and looked up to her bright window. She could see

Stephen up there, waving a spatula in front of the mirror over the dinner table. She climbed the steps and threw open the door on the last note of *Die Meistersinger.* "I see you picked my lock again!"

Stephen stuck the spatula under his arm and sighed. "Thank you very much," he said to the mirror. "I'll be available for autographs after dinner. But my guest is here and dinner is ready, and it is now time to eat."

Virginia snickered. "It smells good. What did you make?"

"Chicken Something. I put flowers on the table," he said, "and candles. We're all ready. Go sit down, Ginny."

"I have to wash." In the bathroom, she held her hands under hot water. Supposedly it cured a headache. A needlepoint hung on the wall by the sink: "Let your light so shine before men, that they may see your good works, and glorify your Father which is in heaven." Mrs. Viksma had put it there. Virginia looked up at the rows of bulbs over her mirror. Three of them were burnt out.

"Dinner's getting cold," called Stephen.

"I'm coming."

The kitchen was dark when she came in, except for a fluttering candle. He pulled out her chair, and she sat down. She opened her napkin and looked up to say something, but he had his eyes closed.

"Amen," she said when he opened his eyes.

They served themselves and ate quietly for a little while, just glancing at each other. He was handsome in the half-dark. That you had to say for him.

"You seem very peaceful tonight," he said cheerfully. "You must have had a good day at work. Usually you're ranting and raving about exclamation points."

"Dr. Katharde hardly spoke to me this afternoon. I'm not peaceful, just sleepy. What did you do with yourself today?"

He sat forward in his chair. His eyebrows shifted around while he thought. "Not much. It was your average boring day in the university library. I started a paper, read some dusty old books, drove home, and cooked you dinner."

"Do you ever get lonely, Stephen?"

"I'm too busy for that."

Virginia held her finger close to the candle flame, as close as she could stand. "Sometimes I feel lonely. I can be talking to somebody I know really well, and I get this overwhelming feeling that I'm by myself. I'm a stranger."

He took another bite.

"Stephen."

"What?" He kept chewing.

"Stephen, I've been meaning to talk to you about something."

"Uh-oh."

"It's not what you think."

"You're not going to tell me to get lost?"

"No."

"What is it, then?"

"It's what I just said. I feel disengaged."

"Then let's get engaged."

"Oh, Stephen."

"Virginia, you're always saying you can't stand having me around so much. You need time by yourself. Now you're saying you're lonely."

"I guess I'm not really talking about you and me. It's a religious thing. My religious views have changed."

"What? You're not a Methodist anymore?"

"It's worse than that. This is hard to say, but I might as well start with you. The fact is that, although I haven't worked it out in my mind yet, I find that I simply don't believe anymore."

"Believe in what?" He looked at her, chewing steadily.

"In God."

He stared.

"Why are you looking at me like that?"

"How do you expect me to look?"

"I don't know. You look hurt."

"That's a pretty shocking announcement, Ginny. Of all the things to decide." He balled up his napkin and threw it across the table. It landed in her lap.

"Don't take it personally. It's been coming for a while; I just didn't know how to explain it to you."

"Well, try. Explain to me exactly how you became an atheist."

"Well, I was at the University of Chicago. Several months ago."

He put his head in his hands. "While visiting the birthplace of the atomic age, she loses her religion."

"I met a guy," she said.

"I don't like the sound of that."

"I was at the Oriental Museum, and I met this guy who's a mummy expert."

"Now there's a job title women can't resist."

"Actually, he was very attractive. But that's none of your business, Stephen. The important thing is that we talked for hours about religion. He's a Marxist."

"I thought he was a mummy expert."

"He's a Marxist mummy expert, O.K.?"

"He advocates equal embalming for the working class."

"Stephen—"

"Did you kiss him?"

"Stephen. Now, shut up. I don't have the patience. I can't explain what happened to me. We were talking about sin, or at least I was talking about sin, and he was talking about the CIA. Suddenly I was right in the middle of this lie, this *lie,* and I suddenly realized: It's all been a lie. I don't believe any of it."

"What's the lie, Ginny?"

"I told him I was a sinner. As soon as the words were out of my mouth, I knew what a liar I was. I was never a sinner, Stephen. God didn't save me out of anything. I was ten years old when I started going to church. Religion came very easily to me, but it was really just a way of getting out of the house and thumbing my nose at my father. It wasn't true. I realized it for the first time."

"You realized this for the first time while talking to some Marxist Egyptologist?" Stephen's face wrinkled up.

"I guess I didn't *realize* it." She frowned. "I just knew that I knew it. It wasn't a rational thing, because I can think of good reasons to be religious. This was an intuitional thing. I just knew I didn't really believe, not for myself. As soon as I knew it, I felt like I could really breathe for the first time in years."

Stephen rubbed his long nose with the back of his hand. "Maybe you have Christianity burnout. I mean, you've been working for Milton Katharde, reading popular theology all day. It's like eating the same food or listening to the same song again and again. After a while, the thought of it just kind of disgusts you."

She shook her head. "No, once I ate linguine alfredo every night for a year. I don't get tired of many things. This time, I felt like I was walking out of a house where I'd lived most of my life. I can't go in that house anymore."

Stephen was smiling down at his empty plate. He shook his head. "You say you felt free after you stopped believing. But you told me before that you felt free when you first went down the aisle at church."

"As a kid," she said, raising her eyebrows.

"So? You were a kid, so what? I remember just how you said it—you had to fight with your father even to go to church, and he made fun of you, but you knew that because there was a God, there was justice in the world, and the wicked people couldn't go on abusing everyone forever. Remember?"

Virginia nodded slowly. "There is justice. But I shouldn't have invented God. A person can believe in justice without believing in God."

"How? Justice is meaningless if there's no absolute right or wrong."

"All I'm saying is that I don't feel like a Christian anymore, I don't know that Christianity is true, and so I won't believe it. And yes, I suppose that honesty is an absolute. In my little universe, anyway. 'Truth shall not bend the knee to Baal.'"

Stephen shook his hair back and picked up his plate. He picked up hers, too, and went to the sink. "How can you stand not believing?" he said. "How can you stand thinking you're all alone in the universe?"

"I'm not *all* alone. You're here, too."

"Yeah, but for how long? Just till you get tired of me." He looked gloomy.

For a moment she didn't know what to say. "Oh, come on, don't take it all so seriously." She waited, hoping to see his expression change, but it didn't. "I was meaning to ask you, anyway—I had no luck this afternoon Christmas shopping. Would you like to take the train into the city tomorrow and see the Christmas lights?"

"I can't tomorrow."

"Well, how about Sunday?"

"I haven't lost *my* faith, Virginia. I have to go to church."

"Oh well, then." She shrugged her shoulders.

"How about Monday?" he said, glancing back at her.

"All right." They did the dishes, watched television, and he left. She imagined the Viksmas glancing out the window as he strode across the porch downstairs: "There goes that boyfriend again, Harold. Those two are up to trouble."

She closed the door, locked it, and turned off the living-room light. She sat down on a trunk in her bedroom, thinking of her father. That was the only part that got her, the part that almost turned her back to religion—knowing she'd have to hear him say, "I told you religion's a bust. Guess you had to make a fool of yourself to learn what I already knew." He'd turn to her mother as soon as he heard the news and start singing stupid versions of "Just As I Am":

> *Just as I was, without one flea,*
> *until that dog shed hair on me. . . .*

In the kitchen, the phone rang. She had already kicked her shoes off. She padded across the cold maple floor of the living room. Downstairs, Mrs. Viksma's piano paused before the second verse of "O for a Thousand Tongues."

"Hello?" she said.

"Virginia?"

"Hi, Florence!"

"Are you busy? Do you have company? I'm sure I woke you up."

"No. What is it?"

A long sigh crackled over the receiver. "I have a confession to make, Virginia. After our conversation this morning, all I could think about was Christmas, and you not going home, and what Mark said about Milton. I got a little crazy, I guess. Oh, my dear, I hope I haven't gone and done a foolish thing."

"I can't imagine you doing anything foolish."

"I decided that this is the year. The year of the office Christmas party. I've written everyone an invitation. Everyone in the department."

"How nice," Virginia said casually. She opened the refrigerator and took out the orange juice. "What changed your mind?"

"I suppose I'm tired of hearing people call Milton a Scrooge just because he gets a little impatient at this time of year. People who say such things don't know him the way I do."

"I guess you're right." Virginia was thinking that she certainly didn't know Dr. Katharde the way Florence did. "Florence, I don't see anything crazy about that. I think it's nice—"

"But I didn't tell you yet what I've done."

"You said you've mailed invitations to everyone."

"I'll mail them tomorrow, from my home. I wrote them this afternoon and stamped them with Dr. Katharde's signature."

"You did what?"

"I addressed them from Milton. And not only that, but I lied about what the occasion was. I invited each professor to a private meeting on Wednesday night. An *urgent* meeting. Is that a terrible lie?"

"What about Dr. Katharde? How will you tell him he's planned a surprise party?"

"I won't need to. I sent him the same invitation, signed by President Avella, a.k.a. me. And I need you to do something for me, dear."

"What?"

"I need you to decorate the office before Wednesday night. My daughters are here now with the children, and I'm much too busy. I can bake up loads of goodies, but could you go over and make things pretty?"

"Sure. I'm not busy."

"I didn't think you would be, you poor sweet thing. All alone at Christmas—I couldn't stand the thought of you going without any parties or festivities, Virginia."

"So when does the party start, anyway?"

"At 8:30. After that nativity play at Fawcett Chapel, since Dr. Katharde and Dr. Nimitz are both in it. And our party will end promptly at 9:30. Virginia, I must confess I'm quite anxious about this. I worry what might go wrong."

"Nothing we won't live through," said

Virginia absent-mindedly. "Stop worrying and sleep well. I'll see you Wednesday." She put the phone down and shuffled back to her bedroom with a half-empty glass of juice in her hand. Later that night, she woke up cold and got out of bed to fetch an extra blanket. Passing the window, she looked out at the snow falling quietly on the brick patio below. Her cat, Miranda, jumped from a bookshelf to the windowsill and put her warm nose to the pane.

"So what if I'm all alone in the universe?" Virginia said. "Maybe I like it that way." She went to sleep again with no trouble.

3

A Change of Direction

ON MONDAY MORNING, THE CHICAGO
Northwestern train took Virginia and Stephen
through scrubby woods, past dingy warehouses
and shells of railroad cars all the way to the
great canyons of the city. Chicago looked like
a park that day. The temperature had climbed
to a moderate twenty degrees, just warm enough
so that human beings could walk down Michigan
Avenue without wincing. Christmas shoppers
crowded the streets. Bare trees blinked with yellow lights. Live elves tiptoed on soapy snow in
the windows of Marshall Field's. At Water Tower
Place, a hundred Santas on the street clanged
their bells and rattled their full pots—"Thanks,
man, thank you. Help the poor. Thanks, lady."

Virginia bought Stephen a pair of binoculars (his mother had suggested them) but decided against the one-dollar gift wrap because it was too expensive. On the way back to the station, he put his arm around her and said, "Just a minute, I still have to buy your present. You wait here and don't turn around, O.K.?"

"Don't turn around? How long are you going to be?"

"It won't take long."

She turned her back to him but peeked around just long enough to see him put a ten-dollar bill in a Salvation Army pot and run into an expensive jewelry store. Stephen was nothing if not generous. Maybe she should have had his present wrapped, after all.

"Repent or be damned," he said behind her, just a few minutes later. How had he shopped so fast?

"What?"

"That's what the sign says. 'Repent or be damned.'" He pointed up to the paper she'd been absent-mindedly staring at on a nearby telephone pole, a coloring-book picture of Jesus and Mary with those words scrawled at the bottom. "It's a divine message for you," he said.

"And to think I almost missed it." She yawned and started walking again. The sun and the cold wind had stiffened her like a rag on a line. A little while later, taking the 8:40 train home, she longed for a hot bath and a warm bed. She could hardly hold her head up. Stephen's soft shoulder looked so inviting, and yet so fraught with consequences. She leaned forward and put her forehead on the back of the empty seat in front of her.

"I thought we'd have a late dinner," said Stephen.

"Dinner? Oh no, not dinner. I'm going home to bed."

He started whistling "Beautiful Dreamer." They got off the train at College Avenue Station. Two blocks from her apartment, they met a man selling Christmas trees to raise money for Bibles in the Ukraine.

"Hey, let's buy a tree for your apartment," said Stephen. "Got any money left?"

"Are you kidding?" said Virginia. "Not after buying your Christmas present."

"But do you see this big, beautiful spruce? It's only $10.95, and it's for a good cause." He took out his wallet. Before long, they had hoisted the tree onto Stephen's shoulders and pointed him toward the Viksmas' house. He huffed, "Man, I can't see where I'm going with these branches in my face. Hold on to my elbow, will you?"

"Sure." She felt wide-awake now. The spruce smelled sharp and delicious. A wind chime rattled on a tree branch somewhere. After a block Stephen switched the tree to his other shoulder. A few houses down from the Viksmas', he groaned and stopped.

"This is what you get for your generosity," she said.

"Virginia, I can't carry it by myself. I'll hold on to the trunk, and you get the nose."

She stepped ahead and grasped the top of the tree by the needles. "I feel like we're dragging someone away by the hair." She stopped. "I've got an idea."

"What?"

"Let's take this up to my office."

"Your *office*. On the fifth floor of McIlwain?"

"I'm supposed to decorate for our surprise Christmas party Wednesday night."

"Now?"

"Why not? This tree's too big for my apartment, anyway. We can go to dinner after we set it up."

He sighed and changed directions. A block from the college he said, "Here's my folks' house. Why don't I run in and borrow a string of tree lights?" In a moment he was back, with a paper grocery bag full of lights and Christmas balls, crepe-paper streamers, bells, and ribbons. It was beginning to snow. They hurried up the hill to McIlwain, then climbed the west stairs, shedding pine needles all the way. The steps creaked and sagged under their weight.

"Somebody's here," said Stephen. "There's a light on in one of the offices down the hall."

"That's Dr. Erlichson's office." Virginia put her end of the tree down and walked quietly to the office door. "Hello?" she said, pushing it wide open. "Nope," she called out. "He's not in here, must have left his light on. Typical." She closed the door gently and unlocked the door of the main department. Stephen dragged the tree down the hall after her. More needles sprayed over the carpet as he yanked it across the threshold.

"Set it up there in the corner near the windows," she said, "and I'll unravel the Christmas lights." The green cords were bound up in tiny, tight knots. *Like Dr. Katharde's sentences,* she thought. "How did you get your lights knotted up this tight, anyhow?"

"My mother did it. She's very good at knots—no formal training, just natural talent."

"This dratted thing!"

"Shhh, Ginny, you're being kind of loud."

"Don't you people organize things a little before you put them away?"

He smiled. "Give me that; you hang up streamers."

They traded jobs, and Stephen had the knots untied and the lights strung up around the room in ten minutes. Virginia hung streamers from the ceiling, bells from the tree branches, bows on the window shades.

"It looks good," he said. "Too bad we don't have a star for the tree. You know what would be funny? To get that weird mask from the third floor and stick it on top. In place of an angel."

Virginia hesitated. "No," she said, smiling a little at the idea. "It'd be sacrilegious."

He put his hands on his hips. "What do you care?"

"Florence wouldn't like it. It's her party."

"Oh, come on, just for a joke."

"No. We need to get out of here before Dr. Erlichson comes back, anyway. What's left to hang up?" She fished in the bottom of the grocery bag, under old wrapping paper and empty ribbon spools, and put her hand on a pile of mistletoe. "Oh, let's hang this up. That way Abelard and Héloise have an excuse to kiss."

"What?"

"Nothing. I need more tape or tacks or something. Look over there in my desk."

He pulled open her top drawer. "Very neat drawer, Virginia. No tape, though, or tacks."

"Try Florence's desk."

"None here. Does it really matter that much? Do we have to have mistletoe?"

"Of course we have to have it." She found the tacks herself, gave them to Stephen, and went back to hanging bows. When she turned around again, he gave her an arch smile. He had hung the mistletoe over Dr. Katharde's door and was now waiting under it.

"That's not what I had in mind," she said.

He leaned over to her anyway, and she gave him a kiss as dry as bread crust—*not* wanting to get his hopes up. They gathered together the leftovers and went quietly into the hall. Stephen put his finger on his lips, looking up and down. "All clear," he whispered. "Come on." They padded down the hall past Dr. Erlichson's door. Once they hit the west stairs, they ran, and laughed when they pushed through the door at the bottom and stood in the open air again. Snow swirled around them.

"Uh-oh," said Stephen.

"What?"

"I brought those thumbtacks. I don't want them in my coat pocket. The package will come apart, and I'll shred my hand or something."

She looked up to the fifth-floor windows. "Take them back. Just hurry. I'm cold."

She waited for him under the Tower, while the snow came down. In spring, dark green ivy sprouted all over this limestone building. Redbud and magnolia bushes blossomed down the hill. But McIlwain was most beautiful, she thought, on a winter's night like this, against a black sky full of tiny white stars falling, falling, falling.

Stephen came back through the door, smiled brightly, and put his arm around her. "All taken care of," he said. "By the way, am I invited to this party?"

"No," she said, "I'm taking the Egyptologist." They walked down the hill toward town as the last snowflakes fell and the wind changed direction.

4

The Ghost in the Window

THE INVITATION ARRIVED IN HER MAIL-
box on Tuesday afternoon, typed on Dr. Katharde's letterhead and signed with his stamp:

My dear Miss Falls,

I beg your attendance at a meeting of the
most urgent and private nature on the evening of December 21 at 8:30, in my office.
Please do NOT discuss this invitation with
your colleagues.

> With hope of salvation,
> Milton Katharde

She laughed as she read it, imagining Dr. Erlichson, Dr. Nimitz, Dr. Trapp, Dr. Molliby, even Dr. Katharde opening up similar invitations on this same afternoon, each studying his or her own for secret meaning, each wondering what could be so urgent and private (scandal? dismissal?). One more night and they would all creep up to the fifth floor for their private tête-à-têtes, only to knock heads as they reached the department door.

Stephen came for her early on Wednesday night. They took a long walk in the deep snow, somehow ending up north of campus. As they headed back, she slipped her gloved hand into her jacket pocket and curled it around the invitation. A brick sidewalk took them past modern dorms as flat and smooth as card houses to rough limestone buildings erected before the turn of the century. In the middle of the central quad stood a statue of a freed slave with a Bible in his hand. Virginia sat down on a bench beside him to tie her tennis shoes. "My feet are so numb," she said. "I'm walking on stumps." When she looked up again, someone let out a loud, high giggle. Two black boys in bright yellow hats and coats ran by, pointing at the statue. They vanished between two buildings just as the chapel clock chimed 8:30.

"Faculty brats, most likely," Stephen said.

"Takes one to know one." She stood up and followed him through a dark Shade Hall straight on to McIlwain, approaching the big castle from the back.

"Boy, I wish you didn't work five flights up," Stephen said. They climbed the east stairs to the third floor and she turned down the hall as she always did, about to take the longer way up, passing near the mask.

"Where are you going?" he said behind her, his foot on the next flight of steps.

"I always go this way. It's more interesting."

He hesitated strangely. "It's slower that way, isn't it?"

She looked between him and the black hall, then turned back to join him. Even this direct route to the fifth floor had a few twists and turns. They had to cut through a classroom in the center of the building to reach the west hall and the department office. Virginia got to the office first, stepped in, and stopped. Stephen came in behind her and whistled.

Underneath the streamers and lights that they had hung stood a long table decorated with holly and ivy. Silver trays sprawled under the hedge of green, spread with meatballs and smoked sausages, asparagus sandwiches sliced as thin as cigars, tiny quiches in green foil. Gingerbread wise men peeked out among candied orange rinds and marzipan, butter mints, and flakes of white chocolate rolled up like peeling birch bark.

Virginia came further into the room, smiling, looking around. "Florence? . . . I wonder where she is."

"Maybe she went to the ladies' room," said

Stephen. "I'm going to eat one of these meatballs."

"No! Don't."

"Why not? There are plenty." He picked up a red toothpick, speared one, and popped it between his teeth. "Absolutely delicious."

"Don't eat anything else until Florence comes back."

He looked around. "Where would she be? Hiding in a closet, ready to pop out at us?"

"Unlikely," said Virginia.

"That supply closet maybe?" He looked at the Christmas tree they had set up two nights before, and his eyes stopped for a second. "What about in one of these offices?" He tried Dr. Nimitz's door. "This is locked."

"Shhh," she said just then and pointed to the hall. There were footsteps outside, coming from the west wing.

"Party guests?" he whispered.

"I'm not sure."

"Let's surprise them." Stephen grabbed Virginia by the hand and looked around quickly. He yanked her under the mistletoe into Dr. Katharde's office, closed the door all but a crack, and held a finger over her lips. "This'll be good. Just jump out when I tell you to."

"You don't even know these people," she said. "And we won't fool them, anyhow. I left my purse on Florence's desk."

"Doesn't matter. Shhh."

The footsteps came nearer. Slow, hard steps.

Was that Florence coming? Virginia tried to re-member Florence's walk. She thought of those small high heels of hers tapping the floor like poodle toes.

"Dr. Katharde?" a woman suddenly said. "Dr. Katharde?"

"It's Dr. Trapp," whispered Virginia. "Close the door."

"Hello, Lucy," Dr. Katharde called back, from down the hall. "My, what a lovely hat, makes me hungry just looking at it. What brings you up here tonight?"

"What brings me up here?" said Dr. Trapp, uncertainly. "Well, Milton, your message brings me up here."

Dr. Katharde's steps slowed. "My message?"

"Your invitation."

He chuckled. "Are you trying to confuse me, Lucy? I'm here to meet President Avella."

"Dr. Avella?"

Virginia leaned close to Stephen. "Let's go out."

"Not yet," he said. "Timing's not right."

Dr. Trapp gasped. "Gracious, goodness, mercy, Milton! Come here!" A pause followed.

"What?" Dr. Katharde said. His steps has-tened, then stopped.

"It's a party," said Dr. Trapp happily. She breezed past Dr. Katharde's office door. Through the keyhole Virginia glimpsed a red dress and broad-brimmed hat overflowing with fake fruit.

"Are you responsible for this?" asked Dr. Katharde in a low voice.

"Milton, please."

"Who's responsible?" His voice cracked. "I don't understand. Who?"

"It's not a Roman orgy, Milton. It's just a few hors d'oeuvres and decorations."

Virginia put her hand on Stephen's arm. "Forget timing. Let's go out." He lifted his hand to the knob but stopped as Dr. Trapp sighed loudly outside.

"For heaven's sake, Milton, are you leaving? I don't nurse old wounds, must you?" Her steps echoed after his on the hollow floor outside, then they were gone, probably down the west staircase.

"Now," said Virginia. Stephen pushed the door open gently, but suddenly a third pair of feet sounded in the hall from the opposite direction, shuffling and slow. Virginia yanked the door back. They listened as someone entered the office, padded across the carpet, and stopped nearby.

"Could that be her?" whispered Stephen. "Mrs. Treadwell?" he said aloud.

"Shhh," said Virginia. She heard a light whistle a few feet away—*O come, O come, Emmanuel, and ransom captive Israel.* The whistling stopped, and the carpet sighed gently. A shadow fell across the keyhole; then the doorknob turned. She held out her hand but couldn't catch the door as it swung open in front of them.

"Surprise!" said Stephen weakly. Before them stood Dr. Nimitz, small and shriveled in his nativity play costume, a black satin robe and a yellow turban that tilted forwards over his thick glasses. He held one hand over his heart, gripping in it a white envelope that looked exactly like the one in Virginia's pocket. For a moment he said nothing at all. He licked his cracked lips and breathed heavily, looking from side to side and up and down at the tree, the food, the mistletoe. His jaw went slack. "A party," he whispered.

"Don't be upset, sir," Virginia said.

"Don't be upset?" he said hoarsely.

"Florence will be back soon to explain."

"Oh dear," he said sadly, almost in tears. "You don't understand. Where is Florence? She ought to be here. Where is Milton?"

"Virginia," said Stephen, with his hands in his pockets. "Before anything else, I think I need to tell you something."

"What?"

He pulled her back a couple of feet into Dr. Katharde's office and spoke in a low voice, though not out of Dr. Nimitz's earshot. "I hung that mask on the Christmas tree."

She looked blankly at him.

"On Monday night," he said, "I pretended I had to return the thumbtacks, but really I ran upstairs and took the mask out of the case downstairs, and—you know—I hung it on the tree. The weird thing is, it's gone now."

Dr. Nimitz cleared his throat loudly, and Virginia at once saw everything with new understanding. She understood that Florence had come to the office this evening, happily laid out all that dainty finger food, then noticed that *thing,* that mask, grinning eerily in the corner. She understood that Florence had taken the mask back downstairs to its proper place and that probably she was there at this very moment, angrily locking it away under glass.

"I should have let you shred your hand on the thumbtacks," she said.

"I'll see if she's downstairs," said Stephen.

"No," she said firmly. "I'll go. You stay here with Dr. Nimitz. And above all, don't mention this to Dr. Katharde if he comes back. He's mad enough as it is." She marched out into the hall and turned east, heading for the central stairs.

The darkness wrapped around her as she walked down to the third floor. The central staircase landed just east of the Walford Lecture Hall. When she got to the landing, she took her hand from the cool, solid stair rail and felt her way along the wall of the third floor toward the alcove where the display case sat.

"Florence?" she called out. No reply.

At least she could see whether the mask had been put back. In order to see the case she would need to turn on a light somewhere. She stayed to the right of the hall, feeling past a display of other missionary artifacts (poison darts, tiger teeth, et cetera) for the next doorknob.

"Would all dart-blowing savages please clear the hall?" she said aloud and laughed half-heartedly.

The wall felt as smooth as a mirror, no door-knobs, no door frames. She stood still, staring at the darkness with her hands on her hips. Then she sighed and started walking again, this time spreading both hands out in front of her against the wall, fanning them up and down.

She took a few steps. Nothing.

A few more steps. Nothing.

A little further.

"Yow!" Her foot slung forward like an arrow. Down she went. Big pain.

She fell onto her side, and her forehead smacked into the wall. Bigger pain. Scrambling to her feet, she fumbled again for a doorknob. *Find one, find one. There!*

As she threw open the door, a curtain of blinds clattered against the glass. She put her hand on a light switch, then stepped back into the hall, blinking in the brightness.

"Good Lord," she whispered into the quiet. "Why?"

Someone had smashed the glass mask case to pieces, shattered it to thin shards, leaving nothing but the wooden shelves and frame. Glass sparkled all over the floor. At the center of the whole violent mosaic lay the mask. The *mask*. She wanted to move away, to run, but she couldn't take her eyes off the bright triangles of broken glass arranged like rays around that calm face.

She took a step back and nearly tripped over something behind her. A hammer lay in a puddle of red.

"Blood!" Virginia shrieked and jumped forward, horrified. It was on her shoes. She reached down to rub it off, and her stomach wrenched as she touched it, sticky and cool. She started past the lecture-room door toward the steps. Just then she heard a noise ahead of her. The tall oak door of the lecture room unlatched and swung open.

"No!" she screamed.

A black hood and a billow of black cloth swooped out of the dark room. A man grabbed her around the arms. She wriggled and kicked blindly. The sole of her tennis shoe hit something.

"Stop it!" he yelled. His hands relaxed for a second. She went limp, fell, and rolled sideways as hard as she could. Glass crunched underneath her.

"Listen to me! Listen to me!" His voice was deep, rough.

Virginia clambered away, shrieking. She tripped up the short steps in the middle of the hall, ducked around the corner, and scrambled on all fours up two flights of steps. *He's behind me, he's behind me, he's behind me.*

"Ginny!" Stephen was already halfway down the stairs to meet her. His face was white. "What happened?"

She grabbed his hand and charged past him, yanking him up behind her. "I have to—I have to call the police."

"Slow down! What's going on?"

The other professors had come up to the top of the stairs. Dr. Katharde and Dr. Trapp had returned from wherever they'd gone. Dr. Nimitz stood close to Dr. Trapp, holding his turban. They all had a look of helpless horror.

"There's a man down there!" Virginia yelled. "Downstairs!"

"Who was it?" said Dr. Katharde, coming suddenly to life. "What did he look like?"

"He's wearing a . . . a robe or something. I didn't see his face."

"He'll try to leave the building. We better find out which way he goes—Lucy, you take Miss Falls to the office, lock the door, and call the police. We men will spread out quickly and watch from the windows—Edward, go over to fifth east and see if you can see anyone from the stairwell windows."

"From the stairwell?" said Dr. Nimitz weakly. "Are you sure?"

"Hurry up, Edward!"

"I'm not looking out any window," said Stephen, charging back down the staircase. "I'm going after the jerk."

"Wait!" called Dr. Katharde, but Stephen leaped down the stairs and disappeared around the corner. Dr. Katharde shook his head and hurried away toward the west wing. Dr. Nimitz rubbed his bald head, then started through the empty classroom that divided the two wings of the building. He stopped in the door, trembling too hard to flip on the light switch. "Lucille," he said in his thick falsetto. She held her hat on and went after him.

"Where are you going, Lucy?" said Virginia. "Dr. Katharde told us to stay."

"I have to stay with Edward. I'll be back—go in the office and lock the door."

Virginia stayed another second in the hall, catching her breath, feeling stranded. They had all left her so quickly. And then she looked down at her white shoes, streaked red, and realized, *That may be Florence's blood.* She ran back and slipped into the department, shaking. *Don't panic,* she thought. She turned the lock and switched off the lights so as not to attract the attention of anyone—*him*—passing through the hall. Then she went into Dr. Katharde's office and pulled his door shut behind her. The arched windows were bare over his table, but it was still dark up here, above the streetlights. Blood rushed in her ears. She called the police, reported the attack, then hung up and dialed Florence's home number.

"Yes?"

"Florence! It's you, isn't it! That's you!" Her voice trembled. She was hoping—

"No, this is her daughter Merrel."

"Oh." . . . *Why couldn't it be her?* . . . "Is she there?"

"No, she's not. Who's speaking, please?"

"Do you know where she is?"

"She's at the college. Can I take a message?"

"No, thank you." Virginia put the phone down

and turned to look out the window over north campus. The lawns, the sky were peaceful. Fawcett Chapel was still lit up to the west. Closer to McIlwain, a woman hurried across the sidewalk in front of the conservatory. A pair of children crossed her path and raced across the snow, through circles of light cast by lamps. After a few minutes two men appeared from around the chapel and took the children's hands; then the four of them walked up the sidewalk to the brick path around McIlwain. Virginia wanted to lean out and shout, "Danger! Don't come near here!" But the words would be lost. She felt like a ghost leaning out the window, looking at the living.

"Hey!" someone shouted directly underneath her. It was Dr. Erlichson, standing by a car.

She cranked the window open. "Don't come in! Go home!"

"I'm here to meet Milton," he shouted back, "and I forgot my key to the building. Can you let me in?"

"I can't come downstairs. There's a man in the building."

"Virginia, my wife is on her way to one of those make-up parties. Throw me a key, or she might lose the pink Cadillac."

"Not right now, I said. You should probably go home."

"Come on, I'm cold."

She shook her head and closed the window, but went for her keys. She tossed them out the window behind the refreshment table. "If you have to come in, come straight upstairs!"

"Don't throw them in the holly!" he said as his wife's car pulled quickly away.

A knock rattled the door to the hall. "It's just me," called Lucy Trapp. "I'm letting myself in." Dr. Trapp's hat brushed the door frame as she stepped quickly into the room. A plastic strawberry dropped onto her shoulder and then to the floor, but she didn't notice. Dr. Nimitz came in after her, and she locked the door behind them. "We were hoping Florence would have come back," she said.

"Well, she hasn't come back," said Virginia. She rubbed her arms where the man's hands had burned her. "Neither has Stephen, and neither has Dr. Katharde."

"They need our prayers," said Dr. Nimitz, sounding distressed. He sat in a chair and began to clean his glasses vigorously with the hem of his robe. The lobes of his ears shook. Dr. Trapp sat down at Florence's desk and closed her eyes. She touched the bridge of her nose with the back of her hand. Was she going to cry? Virginia couldn't stand to look. She got up nervously and went to the window again. Dr. Erlichson had disappeared, but the police had pulled up, their blue-and-red lights disturbing the white calm outside. From the northwest door came Dr. Katharde to meet the officers, holding a big book under one arm that Virginia thought was probably a Bible. Stephen marched behind him,

looking all around and glancing anxiously up to
the fifth floor.

Virginia wished she could wash her shoes.
She wished she could remember that face, that
face against the dark. She wished Florence
were here.

5

Detective Deacon

THE NEXT MORNING, VIRGINIA TURNED off her alarm just as a big December wind screamed across the house, lifted the rafters, and dropped them. *Thunk.* She hadn't slept at all. The police had taken her home (shoeless) after an hour of questions that she couldn't even remember now, and she'd sat for another hour erect on a hard corner of the couch, shivering. How could she ever close her eyes again; how could she let the darkness swirl around and not think that a door might open somewhere, unleashing shadows, releasing nightmares into flesh and blood?

She put her clothes on and headed straight out, avoiding the railroad path by a block, passing Stephen's house without so much as glancing at his window. It was a beautiful day. The air was brilliant and cold, and she had to fight the natural lift in her spirits. Just up the hill sat the Tower, shining like a gravestone in the sun. Underneath it, a small crowd of blue cars huddled near a larger crowd of vans. The world had changed overnight. Emmet College had been invaded. She kept her eyes on McIlwain as she trudged through the snow. A blue cap moved across Dr. Erlichson's west-wing window and disappeared.

At the northwest door a guard stood sipping coffee. She recognized him from the night before. In his sunglasses she saw her tiny self looking down nervously, her hair flapping on her straight neck. "I'd like to know whether you've found Florence Treadwell."

"You're the girl who got assaulted last night, right?"

She nodded, not wanting to.

He chewed at his lower lip. "Yeah, I was there when you gave your statement. You're lucky you didn't get killed last night, you know that? Deacon said—"

"I want to speak to the officer in charge."

"That's Deacon."

"Who's Deacon?"

"Detective. Fifth floor. I'll let him know you're coming."

She moved by the guard, feeling his eyes on her. Climbing the stairs to the fifth floor, she walked through dark into light and into dark again. On the third floor she heard rumbling, thumping, hammering. A man met her at the top of the steps wearing a black polyester suit and no badge. His orange hair glowed like the last bite of a Popsicle. His ears stuck straight out.

"Are you a policeman?" she asked uncertainly. "Deacon, is it?"

He nodded and pointed a thumb down the hall toward the theology department. "Come into my office." She followed him to the office and looked around sadly. The place was a wreck. Books and papers lay in scattered heaps across the floor. The streamers and signs were gone. The party table had vanished. All of this had happened in just a few hours. Only the Christmas tree remained as it had been the night before, silvery green and glowing with lights. She looked across the office at the window where she had thrown the keys to Dr. Erlichson.

"Are you finished with my shoes yet?" she said.

"We'll keep them for a while," said Deacon. "If you don't mind."

"How about Florence? Have you found her?"

"Have a seat, Miss Falls."

Virginia sat down in a chair near the door. The detective sat down on Florence's desk and swung his leg over the side, childishly. The drawers were gone. The holes gaped open. "Best-case scenario, Miss Falls: I think Mrs. Treadwell's been kidnapped."

She felt a chill run up her neck. "O.K.," she said hoarsely. "And what about the worst case?"

71

"It's hard to figure out what anybody would have against a lady like that. She doesn't have money. From talking to some of your colleagues I get the idea she didn't even know many people outside the college. You know who her close friends were, Miss Falls?"

"No." She thought of the few times she'd seen Florence elsewhere—in the grocery store, buying ground pork ("Surprise them with ground pork!" Florence had read from the package, and laughed), in the parking lot of Campus Church on Sunday morning (Virginia had been on her way to buy a newspaper), and once at a band concert in the park with a group of church ladies, her flowered print dress billowing in a spring breeze. She and Florence were too different to be friends outside this building. Their lives had only converged in McIlwain.

"I don't know much about Florence," Virginia said, "except that she's a good person."

"Yeah, well, aren't they all. How about her ex-husband?"

"I thought she was a widow."

Deacon frowned. His freckles gathered under his eyes. "Professor Katharde, he says she's divorced, doesn't say much else. She have any enemies at the college?"

Virginia shook her head. "The man I met in the hall wasn't from the college. I know that for sure."

"How do you know? It was dark."

"I just *know.*" She looked up stubbornly, feeling like she might cry, not wanting to make a fool of herself. "Emmet College people don't do things like this."

He shrugged. "What I want to ask you about," he said, "is the Christmas party. Who knew about it?"

"Florence and I, and Stephen."

"That would be Stephen Holc." He looked at a notepad lying on the desk beside him. "The guy who tried to chase your attacker last night."

"Right."

"Your boyfriend?"

"No."

He raised his eyebrows. "And the others— Katharde, Erlichson, Nimitz, and Trapp—they all thought they were invited to a meeting."

"Yes. And Dr. Howard Molliby. I don't know where he was last night. He was invited, but he didn't come."

Deacon scribbled quickly. "Whoever abducted Mrs. Treadwell knew she'd be here last night setting up between about 7:30 and 8:30. Someone obviously gave him that information. Either you or Mr. Holc tell anybody else about that party?"

Virginia thought a minute. "It's possible that the president of the college knew. Virginia signed Dr. Katharde's invitation with his name."

"Dr. Avella," said Deacon with obvious interest, picking up the notepad. He tapped the side of Florence's desk with one heel. "I talked to him this morning—said he didn't know a thing. Nobody else?"

"Not unless Florence told her family. But why did her kidnapper have to know about her being here, anyway? Maybe she stumbled into a robbery, and the robber had to kidnap her."

"Nothing much to steal down there," said Deacon. "The mask was the only thing in that case, and it's not valuable."

"But since the glass was broken—"

"That may have been an accident. I think he used the hammer on *her,* primarily. It's at the lab, along with your shoes. I'll have a report on that later."

She nodded slowly.

Deacon sat quietly for a second, shaking his head gently. "You know where we found Mrs. Treadwell's keys?"

"Tell me."

He rattled a set of keys in his pocket. "Dr. Mark Erlichson had them. He claims they were thrown to him last night by you, Miss Falls." Deacon smiled, but he twisted up his pale eyes, looking at her ever more intently. "Claims he left his own at home and was unable to enter the building. You threw him these, but they don't open the building."

Virginia shook her head. "Uh," she said, a little nervously. "That's not true. I threw him my keys. That's the only set I keep in my purse."

"So I guess you slept on the sidewalk last night, huh?"

"Meaning . . . ?"

"He didn't give you your keys back, so you must have been locked out at home."

"No, by then I had my keys—"

"Do you remember Dr. Erlichson giving them back?"

She shook her head more vigorously. "I guess not. But I have no idea how an extra set got in my purse."

"Well," said Deacon, "one possibility is you took them from Mrs. Treadwell last night, for some reason I don't know about yet."

She opened her eyes wide. "Are you trying to say I'm a suspect?"

"I just want to know where you got those keys."

"Get real, Detective. *I'm* the one who was attacked. I reported the crime. I came up here this morning without anyone asking me to. Somebody must have put those keys in my purse while I was down on the third floor."

"Who?"

"I don't know. Somebody with good intentions. Maybe they found the keys on the floor and stuck them in my purse by mistake. It was sitting on Florence's desk."

He looked down and wrote.

"How did *you* get those keys, anyway?" she asked. "That's important, isn't it? I mean, did you ask Dr. Erlichson for them, or did he volunteer them?"

"Oh, he volunteered them last night when we

questioned him. Said he thought he'd borrowed that same set before from Mrs. Treadwell." Deacon stood up and paced and looked out the window at the conservatory. "I'm Catholic, myself. You fundamentalists make me nervous. None of you smokes or drinks or says 'poopy.' But a woman disappears and everybody's playing musical keys and everybody's on my back. I got a call this morning from Avella. He says to me, 'Detective, can you imagine what the alumni will say if you investigate the staff or faculty of this college?'" Deacon sat down again. "I told him I'm not protecting a college, I'm catching a criminal."

Virginia dropped her eyes and stammered. "We're not fundamentalists. Was it Florence's blood downstairs?"

"Yes. We think so, at least. She had a fairly rare type."

She swallowed hard. "Will we find her? Has she been murdered?"

Deacon shook his head slowly. "I couldn't say yet. There's no corpse. He hit her over the head with a hammer; she bled a little bit. That's all I know."

"And those keys of hers," said Virginia. "The ones that Dr. Erlichson gave you, what do they go to?"

"They go to Mrs. Treadwell's car, stuff around the house. A few we haven't identified."

"But she didn't have a key to McIlwain." Virginia looked across the dark blue carpet, thinking. She stared at a dust bunny and a little pile of sawdust where a bookshelf had been moved—there must be a mouse around here somewhere. Florence would die if she knew. *Bad joke.*

"Miss Falls," said Deacon, "do you have your purse with you?"

"Huh?" Virginia shook her head to clear her thoughts. "It's at home. You want it, don't you? To see if that McIlwain key is still in it."

"Worth a look." He stood up and rolled forward on his toes. "You drive here?"

"No, I walked."

"Too cold to walk. I'll run you home, myself, but I've got to make a quick call to my wife first. Where's my phone?" As he looked around, something made a chirping sound on top of a filing cabinet across the room. "Well," he said with a laugh, "speak of the devil, and she dials your number." He trotted over, scooped up a long black raincoat, and unfolded a phone from the pocket. "What's up?" His voice dropped. "Come on, baby. Come on, I'm at work here. No, your mother can't come for the whole week. I'd rather spend the week in the jail." He glanced at Virginia. "Pardon me." He stepped out into the hall and shut the door behind him.

Suddenly, strangely, the office phone rang. It rang on Florence's personal extension. Someone out there imagined a secretary at a neat desk, working right through the vacation. The button blinked mournfully. Virginia plucked up the receiver. "Department of Theology. Emmet College."

"Is this Emmet College?" asked a young male voice.

"Uh huh." Answering phones, she was awful at it.

"Can I speak to Florence—uh—Treadwell? Is she available?"

Virginia glanced at the door. "Um, who's speaking, please?"

"This is Lyle Pennyburger at Grand Rapids Bank and Trust?"

She sat down. A big machine rumbled one floor below. It sounded like an oversized dentist's drill.

"Well, Mr. Pennyburger, Mrs. Treadwell's not available. However . . ." Maybe she should let the call go. "I'm her personal secretary, and I do handle all of her, you know, affairs." Too late.

"Oh, man." Lyle Pennyburger cleared his throat. "I've got a check here?"

Everything this guy said was a question. She waited, flipping her Roll-a-Deck back and forth with her pinkie. "Yes, what about it?"

"The check is not," he said, "going to clear because, like, there's only a balance of twenty dollars in her account? That doesn't cover it?"

"When was the check written, um, Lyle?"

"Yesterday."

"Yesterday." *The day of the kidnapping.* Virginia bounced in her chair. Where was Deacon?

She picked up a stapler and hurled it at the door. "Now tell me," she said sweetly, "to whom was the check made out? Where was it cashed, et cetera?"

"Oh, like, I'm not sure I should say—I mean this has never happened any of the other times? The money usually comes in first?"

"Other times? What are you talking about?"

There was a long pause, then a loud breath into the receiver. "I guess, like, I should wait and speak to Mrs. Treadwell? I'll call back later?"

"No!" Virginia pushed her Roll-a-Deck off the desk. It was empty anyway. "Actually," she said. "Mrs. Treadwell is *very* particular about her finances. I perhaps should, no, I *definitely* should discuss the matter with the head of your bank now."

The third floor rumbled. She licked her teeth nervously.

"He's out for the rest of the holidays, unfortunately? See—"

The door opened across the room. Deacon came back in, kicking the stapler casually out of his way.

Virginia motioned wildly. "I see," she said as Deacon picked up carefully on the other phone.

"O.K., I have a pencil now. You said your name is Lyle Lingenfelter?"

The young man snickered. "I'm Lyle *Pennyburger* from Grand Rapids Bank and Trust. And I was just calling to inform Mrs. Treadwell, you know, about this check? Should the bank cover it, or do we, like, stop payment, or what?"

"Good question. And I'll certainly have her call you as soon as she gets in. Your number, please?" She wrote it down on a ledger pad, then dropped the receiver without saying good-bye. She pressed it back against the cradle, hard, as though she were staunching a wound.

Deacon hung up the office extension and un-folded his own phone. He turned his back to speak into it. "This is Deacon—I want you to trace a call for me—" After a moment he snapped the phone shut and came over to collect the scrap of yellow paper. "Thanks, Miss Falls. This could lead to something, who knows? Listen, why don't you find your own way home? There are six reporters waiting to talk to me, not to mention a federal agent with an attitude. The FBI gets in on these cases after twenty-four hours, just in case the victim crosses state lines."

"Detective," said Virginia.

"Yeah?"

"Please don't tell anyone it was me. I mean, don't let anyone know I got attacked last night."

"You embarrassed, Miss Falls?"

She nodded.

"All right." He scratched his head. "Funda-mentalists, you think the world's so evil, but you never want to talk about the nitty-gritty. Your secret's safe with me."

"I'm not a fun—" Virginia's voice trailed off as the door swung closed behind him. It didn't matter what he thought, anyway.

6

Maybe He Was Too Friendly

OUTSIDE, A SMALL FLOCK OF REPORTERS had hatched from the vans on the front lawn. Virginia avoided them and took the path to Shade Hall, home of Ye Olde College Coffee Shop, twenty yards northeast of McIlwain and up a short flight of cement steps that jutted from a mound of snow. As she started through the door, two boys came running out with tall Styrofoam cups, the same boys she'd seen the night before in the quad. "Did you get Uncle Harold's decaf?" yelled a sharp-voiced woman sitting in an old black Dodge in the side parking lot. *Mrs. Viksma.*

Virginia jumped inside, out of sight. What was Mrs. Viksma doing on campus? And with a couple of young boys? By the time Virginia got to the window with the best view of the parking lot, the Dodge had pulled away. She shrugged her shoulders, went to the snack bar, and ordered a cup of coffee. The shop was empty except for the cashier and a woman slumped over in a booth against the far wall. Something looked familiar about her. Virginia walked over slowly.

"Lucy?" she said, surprised. Dr. Trapp sat up. She'd been crying. She wore no hat, but her hair, matted to her head, looked like a gray bathing cap. Virginia put the coffee down in front of her. "I didn't recognize you without your hat. This is for you, I guess."

"They think Florence has been kidnapped," said Dr. Trapp slowly.

"I know. I just talked to the police."

Dr. Trapp slumped back down. She fished a Kleenex out of her coat pocket and rubbed her eyes with it.

"You look very tired, Lucy."

"I sat up with Edward most of the night. I don't know what to do for him. He's so upset. I don't know what to do."

"What do you take in your coffee—sugar?"

"Oh, dear God," sobbed Dr. Trapp. "That reminds me of Florence!" Virginia went quickly for sugar and cream. From the booth behind her came wild, gulping cries, giant hiccups. Too bad Florence *wasn't* here. She'd have skipped the coffee and comforted a weeping woman.

When Virginia came back, Dr. Trapp had quieted down, but her eyes looked like wedges of pink grapefruit. "You must think I'm crazy," she said.

"No, you're just upset."

"I'm very angry about this, Virginia." She spat out the words. "That anything bad should happen to the kindest person in the world. I think—I believe Florence has suffered enough in her life. Don't you?"

Virginia hesitated. "I guess so." She didn't really know. *But I want to know,* she thought.

"She's suffered enough. She's endured her portion."

Virginia sighed. "What exactly *was* her portion, Lucy?"

Dr. Trapp let out another sob and wiped her eyes. "We shouldn't talk about that."

"I guess I'm wondering about something." Virginia lowered her voice. "The police detective told me just now that Florence is divorced. But she never mentioned it to me."

"Did you expect her to publicize it?"

"No, of course not."

"It was nobody else's business, Virginia."

"I understand that. I just wondered if anyone knew her husband."

"I knew him a long time ago. He taught at the college when I was an undergraduate. I took one course under him, but we only spoke once, and he wasn't friendly. Or maybe he was too friendly. Oh—" Dr. Trapp waved her hand.

What was she waving at? "Anyway, I didn't like him at all."

"What did he teach?"

She sat up. "Don't ask me to discuss him, Virginia. I don't know anything else about him."

"Obviously you do. It sounds important, come on."

"Why don't you ask Milton about him? They were close friends. He's got Florence's daughters staying at his house now."

"Maybe I will."

Dr. Trapp sniffed, looked around, and stood up. "Virginia, I have to go to Edward now."

"Let me walk you home."

"No! Like I told you, talk to Milton." Dr. Trapp stood up and swept a shawl around her shoulders, a lacey black thing. "Goodbye," she said, and then, more ominously. "Take care of yourself. I learned a long time ago that you can't trust anyone else to do it."

"Goodbye," said Virginia. She watched Dr. Trapp clop off in her large black heels, then finished the coffee herself and left by a different door. To avoid the police and reporters, she took the same route home that she and Stephen had taken the night before. The walk seemed longer this time.

When she finally got to the Viksmas, her lips were so numb that she couldn't tell if her mouth was closed or open. She reached the house and tiptoed past the black Dodge and up the steps to her apartment, hoping Mrs. Viksma wouldn't hear her and pop out onto the porch: "Virginia, I've just been up to the college and heard the terrible news. There's a madman on the loose!" No sign of any children around. Maybe they'd gone home, or out somewhere with Mr. Viksma. A brown patch in the snow marked the spot where his truck usually sat.

At the top of the steps, her door stood slightly ajar. She had locked it, she was sure. But someone had opened it, and opened the bathroom curtains. "Who?" she whispered. She could hear the heat going full-blast inside. Was someone in there right now, watching for her, waiting for her?

She took a step backwards, putting her hand out for the stair railing, getting ready to shout for Mrs. Viksma.

"Hey, Ginny!" called a voice from the bathroom window. Stephen wiped a circle on the glass and pressed his nose to it.

"Stephen!" she shouted angrily. "Stop picking my lock, O.K.?"

He cracked the window an inch. "Sorry. I borrowed your tub."

"My tub!" she said. "My bathtub?"

"My mother's giving all the dogs a bath. Where have you been, anyway? I've been trying to call you all morning."

"Stephen, get your clothes on before Mrs. Viksma decides to pay me a visit. I have to look for something." She let herself in, then went straight to her bedroom, where her purse sat on chair.

Stephen came in a minute later as she was scattering the contents over her unmade bed, turning the purse itself inside out, upside down.

"It's not here," she said.

He rubbed his wet head with the bottom of his t-shirt. "What are you looking for?"

"A key. I talked to the police this morning. They say that the key ring I threw down to Dr. Erlichson last night was Florence's—only it was missing the key to McIlwain. I can't figure how I got Florence's keys to begin with."

"Hmm." Stephen lay down on the bed. "Hi kitty." Miranda jumped on his chest and settled against his chin. He stroked her slowly. "You know, I've been thinking. Maybe the guy who kidnapped Mrs. Treadwell is actually angry at her boss. Maybe it's somebody getting even with Katharde by kidnapping his secretary. Anybody up there mad at him?"

"In the department? No way."

"What about those atheists he talks to? He must offend some of them, trying to convince them to become Christians."

"I can't see anyone being that sensitive about religion."

"No? Guess you've never heard of the Crusades." Stephen raised his eyebrows. Downstairs the Viksmas' piano plunked out, note by note, *We three kings of Orient are. Bearing gifts, we traverse afar. . . .* From outside came the dull scrape of a snow shovel. *Mr. Viksma must be back,* thought Virginia.

"Warm in here," Stephen said after a minute.

She nodded. "The Viksmas like it hot. Reminds them of Africa."

"You ever thought of going to Africa, Virginia?"

"No," she said absently. She was considering. Could Dr. Erlichson have lied about the key—could he have taken it off the ring himself for some reason? Why had he been at McIlwain the night she and Stephen went to decorate, anyway? It wasn't like him to work late.

The music downstairs changed to something like a lullaby. Miranda began to purr. Virginia slumped down and started to describe her conversation with the bank clerk, but her words got mixed up with the music, and soon she stopped talking and listened. She felt her elbows and shoulders relax, drift apart. She closed her eyes, and in the darkness of her own mind she had a vision of a man sitting down, facing the other way. He said to her, "Look at me, look at me," but when she came closer, she saw that he was wearing the mask. She opened her mouth to scream, and the cold bedspread hit her like a slap. She sat straight up in panic. "Stephen!"

"What? Huh?"

"I was having a bad dream. Why did you let me go to sleep?"

"I didn't know I was in charge."

She stood up, nervously. "Well, I've got to do something, I can't just lie here."

"Where are you going?"

"I'm going to go see Dr. Katharde. Lucy Trapp told me to go see him."

"Listen, I'll go with you."

"No." She looked around for her coat. "I'll be all right. You better dry your hair before you catch a cold."

"And then what am I supposed to do?"

"Make yourself useful. Search for Florence." Virginia went out and hurried down the steps outside.

"Afternoon," Mr. Viksma called to her from the porch below, leaning on his snow shovel. His blue truck sat in the driveway now, behind his wife's car. He started toward her, walking gingerly down his own icy steps.

"Don't run, you'll fall!" she called back and kept walking quickly away from him. She broke into a trot.

"Virginia—"

"Sorry, but I'm late. I'll talk to you later." It was too cold to stop and chat, and anyway, she wasn't in the mood. She hurried along the stretch of snow beside the sidewalks, dodging around trees, pulling her jacket tight around her neck and shoulders. She wanted to forget that dream. At Harrison's Grocery she bought a hefty roast chicken from the deli. She bought potato salad, too, and coleslaw, as if she were stocking up for a picnic. Leaving the store, she passed the Christmas-tree man on his old milk box. "Lord Bless!" he called out, and she considered for just a second calling back, "Hare

Krishna," but instead she started for Dr. Katharde's house with a heavy grocery bag in her arms.

Though she didn't remember Dr. Katharde's exact address, she recognized his silver Volvo in the carport of a small brick house set back from the road. Two other cars sat in the driveway. *Those must belong to Florence's daughters,* she thought. She heaved the bag up to her shoulder, climbed the front steps to his door, and rang the bell anxiously.

The door opened slowly. A thin, middle-aged woman put her head out. "Yes?"

Virginia hesitated. She knew that it was Florence's daughter. She saw Florence's eyes gazing at her through this other face. "I'm a friend of your mother's."

"Oh." The door opened wider.

Virginia wiped her feet and held out the bag. "I brought dinner."

"Dinner?" The woman looked confused. She took the bag, looked at Virginia, and smiled kindly, just as Florence would have. She stepped out of the way. "I'm Merrel. And you are—?"

Virginia stepped in uncertainly. "My name is Virginia Falls. I work for Dr. Katharde. That's how I know your mother."

"I see." Florence's daughter said it smoothly, almost consolingly, as though Virginia were the one in trouble. "You work for Uncle. Won't you come in, meet my sister?"

Virginia followed her down a short hall into

a tiny kitchen where another woman sat peeling carrots. She didn't look up. "Marissa," said Merrel, laying a hand on Virginia's shoulder, "this is Virginia Falls. She works with Mother. She brought us dinner."

The sister nodded and glanced up, but only for a moment. She had a wide, handsome face, unlike her mother's or her sister's, swollen with crying. She wiped her eyes with the back of her hand and continued peeling.

"The children are off with my husband," said Merrel, "or I'd introduce you to everyone. Would you stay and eat a late lunch with us?"

"Oh, no, no, I couldn't. But thank you." Virginia looked at the clock. It was 2:30. She was hungry.

"Is that Miss Falls?" rang out a voice suddenly, from above. It startled everyone. Both girls looked up, and Merrel went to the steps. "Do you want to talk to her, Uncle Milton?"

"Yes. Send her up."

Virginia went slowly past Merrel and up the steps. On the way she glanced at a portrait of Dr. Katharde with his wife—she had seen the same portrait in Florence's top drawer once. It was hard to imagine Dr. Katharde as a husband. Mrs. Katharde looked happy enough. She didn't look as though she'd been *exclaimed* at all day.

"Come," he said from somewhere down the hall. "I'm in my office, here." She peeked into the first two doors on the hall and saw neatly kept bedrooms, empty. The third room was small and dark, but at the far end Milton

Katharde sat crouched over a metal desk, working in the light of a window. He stood up as she came in and gestured to a chair.

"Thank you, sir."

"I'm glad to see you, Miss Falls. I truly am."

She nodded and sat. He dropped back into his chair and patted his bony knees. "I'm preparing some documents for the police—records of Florence's years in the office, evaluations, et cetera. I'm to meet the detectives again sometime today. Would you like a cup of tea?"

She shook her head. "No, thank you, I'm a coffee drinker."

"Instant? I have a little instant in the closet. Just celebrated its tenth birthday."

"No, thank you."

He made himself a cup of tea. The tea bag looked as though it had been used thirty times before. The water blurred pale yellow. She wanted to ask him right away—*Tell me about Florence's husband, Dr. Katharde.*

"Miss Falls," he said, "did you come for counsel? I'm not sure I'm capable at the moment."

"No, sir. I just came to bring dinner for the family."

"Ah," he said, "then you're the one doing the Lord's work. Comforting the troubled."

She shook her head. "Just bringing dinner."

"We need comfort, Miss Falls. It is hard to trust in the Lord at a time like this. It is hard to trust Him when we don't understand His plan. And I confess, I don't understand it."

Had she heard right? Had he just confessed to doubt?

His eyes were on her, brown and deep. "I don't even desire to read the Word of God, Miss Falls."

"No?"

"Because the Word of God is bitter medicine. If you swallow it, you lose the world. If you do not swallow it, you lose your soul."

"I see." So he didn't doubt. He only admitted that it was hard to have faith.

"Do you agree?" he said.

"Excuse me?"

"Miss Falls, 'the heart of the prudent getteth knowledge; and the ear of the wise seeketh knowledge.'"

Virginia gave him a puzzled look. Why did he always have to talk like a Christian fortune cookie? "Dr. Katharde," she said, "actually—"

"If you live by faith," he said intently, "you may die for what you believe. But if you reject faith, you may destroy yourself and those you love."

"Well, I don't know." She sat up in her chair, uncomfortable, feeling as though he wanted her to argue with him. About what? "Actually, there's something I came to ask you, Dr. Katharde. I really wanted to ask you about Florence's husband."

He dropped his spoon into his teacup with a loud clink. Apparently, this wasn't what he'd expected.

"Dr. Trapp mentioned him to me this morning," Virginia went on.

"She did?"

"She told me to ask you about him."

"I see." He coughed. "Well, Miss Falls, I don't know how much to say."

"Dr. Trapp acted as though it was important."

"Perhaps it is. Yes, I've been thinking that, myself." He fumbled for something on his desk, as though he were fumbling for words. "Florence Treadwell is, of course, an old and dear friend of mine. My wife, Lena, may she rest in peace, died a few years ago, but she considered Florence like a sister. And I suppose that I felt similarly about Raymond Treadwell."

"He taught at the college, Dr. Trapp said."

"Yes." Dr. Katharde put his tea aside. "Raymond was a brilliant scholar, you see. But he cared little for worldly success. He came to me because he longed for a brotherhood of Christian scholars. He wanted a community from which to write apologetics, a quiet corner from which to engage skeptics. So I hired him to teach our freshmen, and meanwhile he worked on a book. His topic was the problem of pain. Why God allows the innocent to suffer."

"That's a difficult question." *An impossible one,* she thought.

"Yes. He spent *years* considering it. Meanwhile, he and Florence married. An unusual pair, I thought then. I was *shocked* when they announced their engagement—I'd never even noticed them together. They were the two people, aside from my wife, whom I most depended on. I was to lose my secretary! That was my most immediate thought. I wondered who would type my books."

Virginia smiled. "I can't imagine you without Florence, Dr. Katharde."

"I can't, either. Not now." He shook his head sadly. "In those days, at least at Emmet College, married women stayed home. Florence was happy. She was blessed. After a year she had Merrel. Another two years and she had Marissa. Mrs. Katharde and I, you know—we were never able to conceive. And so we loved those children like our own."

Virginia nodded. So this is why Florence had said he was no Scrooge. He had treated her children so well.

"No father," continued Dr. Katharde, "loved his children more than Raymond Treadwell. Theology was only Raymond's hobby; his heart belonged entirely to his family. You know, I had foolishly considered myself his mentor, but as I began to see his interest slip away, I realized how *utterly* I needed his help. In the clarity and brilliance of Raymond's thought I had seen my own thoughts expanded and illumined. He, for his part, was kind enough occasionally to bring me fragments of his own work. Most of his book is gone now, you know, flung into a fire. But I carry it in my mind forever." Dr. Katharde tapped his head and picked up his tea again. He held the cup against his chest.

"What happened to him, Dr. Katharde?"

"The last Treadwell child, a son, was born thirty years ago this Christmas Day, ten years after my first meeting with Raymond. Can you imagine what they named him? Milton! You see me smile. I have always hated my name because I was named for my uncle, who *spat tobacco.* But this child could have redeemed any name. He was my pride, my wife's joy, his mother's bliss. As for Raymond, the affection that he had for his son was nothing short of idolatry. I couldn't have blamed him, either! The child was a *wonder,* both brilliant and good-natured. A talented young artist and musician. He went everywhere with his father—on his shoulders, on the back of his bicycle. Little Milton used to come along to the diner where we met to discuss theology. I remember it so vividly—a ten-year-old boy staring up from the corner of our booth with serious eyes."

Dr. Katharde laughed. He took a handkerchief from his pocket and wiped his face. "I wish I could say that I was never jealous, but I was indeed jealous. I felt sorry for myself because I wanted a son. I told God that I thought he had blessed Raymond Treadwell inordinately. Not only was he my superior as a scholar, he also had the son I wanted. Well, an old man doesn't show his tears without reason. Forgive my tears, Miss Falls. I try not to remember, but today I must remember. The boy became very, very ill. From a bad case of measles he contracted encephalitis, which destroyed his brain." Dr. Katharde took a deep breath. "It was as though a door had opened in the floor and the boy dropped through it, and then another door opened, and another door, and he dropped farther and farther away. His last days on this earth were a constant misery."

Virginia looked straight at Dr. Katharde. "It's hard to believe in God's goodness after a thing like that happens."

"For some, yes. Florence suffered very much. But she had other children to care for. So she sacrificed her grief for them and recovered. Raymond, though he didn't lose his faith, turned bitter. He kept writing, working himself page by page from a defense of God to a defense of his own bitterness. You see, he never doubted that pain could refine and sanctify a believer. But he *despised* his pain, he *hated* it! He wanted to bring it to an end through sheer will, and he was unable. His suffering grew until he cursed God. He spurned his family. He flaunted his own free will."

Virginia rubbed her arms. She was getting very cold, and listening to Dr. Katharde was like reading one of his manuscripts. "If Dr. Treadwell really believed in God, how could he reject God? Wouldn't he be afraid of hell?"

"God took his child!" he said. "Could you love someone who took the life of your child, even if he threatened you with hell?"

"I couldn't love a God like that, no." *And I don't.*

"I doubt whether anyone, even his wife, ever understood what Raymond had to endure: such a brilliant man wrestling against his own salvation. He suffered alone. Would that he had asked us to pray for him! I'd have pled for the armies of heaven! I'd have preferred my own damnation to his!"

"When did he leave his family?"

"A few months after his son's death, some students came to me, charging that Raymond was a heretic, teaching antibiblical doctrines, using foul language in the classroom. Then a young woman complained to me of a different sort of indiscretion. Raymond had tried to *seduce* her! I confronted him. He swore at me and said he'd *kill* me for making up lies in order to destroy him. I asked him then to leave the college quietly, during the upcoming winter break. Otherwise I'd have had to bring formal charges against him. Instead, he stood up in a college chapel service one day—in front of two thousand students and hundreds of faculty—and he raged against me, said I had wrongly accused him, and that he'd have revenge on us all one day. And then he stormed out of my office.

"On Christmas Eve that year, my wife hosted a party for the department in McIlwain Hall. That may sound strange to you, an office gathering the night before Christmas, but really we were still like a family then, Florence and Raymond and Edward and I, and Howard Molliby. We were a troubled family, but we were a family. At midnight the chapel bells rang out, and I gathered us all for prayer. I don't remember how Raymond had slipped out, but he must have. We closed our eyes. And then we heard a scream. Such a scream. Dr. Molliby ran to the window. A woman walking below shouted to him, 'Fire in the Tower.'

"I ordered the others away, and I ran for the attic door. The door was locked. I kicked at it. I tried to open the lock. Nothing worked. When I finally left the building at the bottom of the east steps, the first person I saw was Florence. Her face was ashen. 'Where is Raymond?' she said. I pulled her along, and we circled the building together, shouting for him, looking up to the windows. He never appeared. The fire was put out. Only a small portion of the attic burned that night, but—" Dr. Katharde shook his head—"Raymond Treadwell was never seen again."

Virginia locked her hands around her knees. "Was he killed in the fire, Dr. Katharde?"

"We thought so for a time." The old professor could hardly speak now. He buried his face in his hands. "A gasoline can was discovered in the attic. Raymond's fingerprints were all over it."

"How horrible."

"Yes, I almost wish Raymond *had* died that day. Then Florence could have gone on with life. Instead she pinned her hope on every little indication that he might still be alive, perhaps living out of the country."

"Every indication?" It was a suspicious word. "Such as?"

"Such as the mask." He raised his eyes to meet hers.

Virginia felt a chill. "The mask from the artifacts case?"

"Yes. A missionary from Nigeria delivered it to her, oh, ten years ago, it's been. He claimed that a man brought it to his church one day and asked him to take it to her on his next trip to the United States. Florence just *knew* that it came from Raymond. She donated it to the college, and we had to put it downstairs in that glass case—" he rolled his eyes—"near the Walford Lecture Hall where Raymond often taught. I wouldn't have it up in the department, you know. I couldn't stand being in the same room with the thing. I sent it over to the library archives for a while, but Florence begged to have it back in McIlwain, and back it came. She went to look at it every day. She took it as a sign that Raymond was alive and that he would return."

Virginia thought of Florence going to look at that mask each day, hoping for her husband's return, never mentioning her hopes to anyone but Dr. Katharde. "What made her think it came from him?"

"Oh, I suppose it looked like Raymond," said Dr. Katharde. His thin mouth barely trembled.

An uncomfortable moment passed, and then he scratched his jaw suddenly and sat up straight. "Well. Is that all you wanted to know, Miss Falls?"

"Yes, sir. I suppose."

"I should be getting these things ready. Don't mention this to anyone, Miss Falls, until I've had a chance to speak with the police."

"I won't." She wanted to ask more, but she stood up and so did he. "Will you be all right, Dr. Katharde? You seem . . . sad."

He sighed. "I am sad, very sad. But it is well with my soul. Go with the Lord, Virginia."

"Thank you." As she turned the corner into the hall, she heard him mumble something else behind her—a prayer, maybe. She passed the portrait of him and his wife again and studied it more closely this time. Mrs. Katharde smiled at the camera, but her gaze drifted toward her husband. He held her hands. They looked happy together.

Virginia left without saying goodbye to the Treadwell daughters. Out under the trees the evening air tasted as cold and sweet as melon. Before she'd walked twenty yards down the sidewalk, a car ground past her through the snow and salt and pulled into the Kathardes' driveway. She squinted to see who it was: Lucy and Dr. Nimitz. She watched them ring the bell and disappear inside.

Back at the Viksmas' porch, she pulled out her keys and hummed *"Adeste Fideles."* The chapel bells rang 4:30 in the distance. Was it only 4:30? It was already dark. The wind had tapered off, and it had started to snow. As she mounted the steps she heard a crunch to her right, someone stepping through the dry winter shrubs.

"Virginia?"

"Stephen!" She dropped her hands as he stepped out of the bushes. "Stop showing up like this!"

Stephen bent over with his hands on his knees, gasping for breath. "I went back up to McIlwain, Virginia. And I saw him."

"Who?"

"Him," he said hoarsely.

7

Handwriting on the Wall

"DO THE POLICE KNOW YOU'RE HERE? Did you call them?"

Stephen didn't answer. He followed her upstairs and fell down on the couch in her living room, holding his head.

"Your mouth is bleeding."

"He hit me."

"You're getting blood on my couch."

"Well," he said slowly, "it's a red couch, isn't it?"

"That's not the point." She picked up the phone and dialed 911. A recorded message whirred on. "Thank you for contacting the Emmet County Police Department. If you have an emergency, press '1' now. . . ."

"I have a dial phone!" Virginia shouted.

"If you are considering suicide and would like to speak to a volunteer counselor, press '2' now. . . ."

"Oh, for heaven's sake."

"If you have a complaint or suggestion, press '3' now. . . ."

"Never mind, I'm dead." She squeezed the receiver and tapped her foot until a mousy voice at the other end said, "This is the operator."

"I need to speak to Detective Deacon."

"Can you hold?"

"No, ma'am, I cannot hold. This is Virginia Falls. I'm calling about the kidnapping at the college."

"One moment."

"Virginia, don't worry about me," said Stephen. "I'll be fide."

"Fide?"

"What?"

"You said you'd be 'fide'?"

"I said 'fine.'"

"You sound weird. Is your nose broken?"

"Ginny, you look like you're about to throw that phone out the window. Your knuckles are white."

"Deacon's office," said a sonorous male voice suddenly from the phone, as if God had broken in. "This is FBI Agent Goodman."

"May I speak to Detective Deacon?"

"I'm assisting Deacon."

She told him what she knew and then hung

up the phone and went straight to the window to wait for the patrol car.

"So do you want to know what happened?" Stephen said.

"Yes." She looked nervously in the direction of McIlwain, wishing that man wasn't out there, still, roaming wild.

"I wanted to find out how a guy could get out of that building without anybody seeing him. I thought I'd take a look from all sides, make sort of a map of what I saw, and pick out the blind spots; then we'd have a better idea of how he got away and where he went."

"The police didn't mind you looking around by yourself?"

"I told the guard at the door I was going up to see Deacon. But I went to the third floor instead, almost to where you saw the case smashed up."

"Was the glass still on the floor?"

"They'd cleaned it up. The mask was back in the case, and there was a guard looking at it, so I snuck to the stairs and kept going up to fifth east, to the stairwell Dr. Nimitz went to last night. I took a good long look out the window, Ginny, and there was just no way a man could have escaped down front campus without being seen. With the snow and the spotlights on the lawn—he'd be so obvious."

"What if he went the other way—north, toward Shade Hall?"

"That's a possibility. I made a note of it, and

then I went over to the west side of McIlwain to check out the views there. I was still up on the fifth floor, just about to walk through the seminar room to get over to the west wing, and I heard voices.

"Some guys, probably a couple of policemen or custodians, were coming up the east stairs down the hall. And I got kind of nervous. The attic door, right there next to the seminar room, was open. I decided to wait in there till the hall was clear again, I guess so I wouldn't have to explain. Anyway, I haven't been up to the Tower for a while, so I thought I'd have a look around. It's amazing. You've never seen it?"

"I don't remember that I have." That was a silly way of putting it. No, she definitely hadn't. College girls went up the Tower either to ring the bell with fiancés or else to watch close friends ring it with *their* fiancés. She'd had few friends at Emmet, none close. Certainly no fiancés.

"Well, there's a lot of old junk around, and graffiti on the walls from over a hundred years ago. I forgot all about what I'd come for, and I was just looking around. I went up to the next level of the attic, where there wasn't a light. Then I kept going up and up, feeling my way along in the pitch dark. I thought it'd be kind of interesting to go up to the bell tower and take a look at campus, you know, from the roof.

"Finally I got to this very cold little room. You couldn't go any farther—at least I felt around and couldn't find a break in the wall. I figured I'd reached the chamber right under the bell, and I started looking around for the ladder. Something brushed right against my face. It was probably the bell rope. But it felt like a spider's web or something." He smiled out of one corner of his mouth. "I guess I jumped and yelled. And then someone else shouted. And then I shouted, even louder. Then a bright light blinded me, and he grabbed me by the collar and flung me onto the floor." Stephen put his fingers over his chest. "I thought I was about to die."

"Why? What did he do to you?"

"He just kept yelling, *'Where's the ladder? Where's the ladder?'* And he was a big guy, tall. You could just tell. I couldn't remember my own name. I should have hit him or something, but I couldn't even see him. I tried to run out of the room, but I couldn't find my way, and he kept shining that flashlight on my face. Finally he threw it down and came after me and grabbed me and banged my head against the wall." Stephen rubbed his head. "And then the ladder to the bell—I bumped into it and grabbed hold of one of the rungs to keep from falling. I did this Errol Flynn thing and jumped on it and kicked him off me, and then before I knew it I had climbed straight up the ladder and pushed open the trap door into the freezing cold, with him right behind me. I didn't look at him. I just saw his hand come out, and I slammed the door on it as fast as I could and then stood there on the door."

"You mean, you stood in the bell tower, on the door?"

"Yes. I think he gave up right away, but I kept standing there. Until I thought I'd freeze to death. Ginny, I was absolutely, totally freaked out."

"And you don't know what happened to him after that?"

"No. I used my shoelaces to tie the door shut from the outside."

"Your shoelaces, Stephen?" She tried not to smile.

"Yes. And there was a hole in the chicken wire around the Tower. I crawled through that, dropped down; then I started crawling and sliding across the roof, over to the west side where there's a fire escape." He paused and yawned. "I had to hang off the roof and drop five feet to reach it. Somebody else had done it—they'd left a rope up there. The police must have been inside with the reporters because no one stopped me. I should have told them right away what happened, but—" Just a slender circle of blue showed around his black pupils.

"You were confused," Virginia said. She put her hand on his back. "Stay awake, O.K.?"

"My head hurts." He opened his eyes.

"Let me see."

"Ginny," he said very slowly, "who's that girl with you?"

"What are you talking about?"

"That girl next to you—she's your spitting image."

"You're seeing double."

"Just kidding." He yawned again. "Why would anyone want to hurt me, anyway? I don't even *know* Mrs. Treadwell, Virginia. He didn't have to jump me like that. He wanted to hurt *me*."

"Maybe he thought you were someone else." She sat there a minute longer, watching him, then stood up and went to the window, wishing an ambulance would come, wishing Deacon would call her. By now the snow was falling heavily, shooting white sparklers around her window frame. A light blinked on in the house across the street just as sirens sounded softly in the distance. A woman came to the window. "Yep," Virginia said, "the neighbors will certainly be calling Harriet Viksma about this one."

It took forever. Had the police made a wrong turn? When a long white squad car finally pulled up to the curb, Virginia turned to Stephen. "I'm going out to the street for a few minutes, O.K.? I don't want the police going to the Viksmas' door. Are you all right?"

He didn't answer right away. "Well," he said finally, "I think I can handle things up here, at least for a few minutes."

"I'll be back."

She bundled up and went out the door without another word. Behind the police car sat an ambulance flickering like a lit candle; a couple of paramedics climbed out and passed her on the stairs as she stood pointing. "He's up there," she said. "I think he has a concussion."

She watched them go. The window of the squad car opened on the passenger's side, and a black man in a dark suit put his head out. "Are you Miss Falls?" His voice was the one from the telephone, though he wasn't the man she'd imagined. He had a calm face, with handsome dark eyes that were half shut.

She went to the window of the car nonchalantly, holding her coat tight around her stomach. "Yes, sir."

"What if you fill in for him, I mean, take me over to the college, explain what happened?"

"Well . . . " She hesitated. "I guess I could."

"You need to say goodbye?"

She hesitated and looked back up at the apartment. "No," she said. "I guess not, not if you all tell Stephen where I've gone."

The agent nodded. His nostrils lifted and sank down again. She climbed into the back seat next to him, unable to remember his last name. *Agent.* Agent what? Some name that had "God" or "good" in it. As they left Virginia's street, the driver rattled police jargon into his radio—radio noises surrounded policemen like static, she thought. They crossed the tracks and saw McIlwain glowing, a giant jack-o'-lantern on the front campus hill. The police were back in full force. The driver took them up to the brick driveway and stopped near the west door.

"Deacon in the building?" called the agent to the guard by the door.

"He's upstairs."

"Tell him Goodman's on his way up."

"Goodman," whispered Virginia to herself. Agent Goodman gestured for her to go ahead, and together they swept through the door and up the west stairs. He had a smooth walk, almost a glide. He climbed the steps as though he were peddling a unicycle, straight-backed and swift. She followed him down the hall, and they looked in at the empty office.

"Hello!" said someone behind them suddenly. "Hold up there!" Virginia turned and saw Dr. Molliby waddling around the corner from the west stairwell, straightening his red bow tie, which sat alert on the collar of his coat. His white goatee hung down just above it, perfectly coifed. In his left hand he held a wad of tissue. She realized as he came in that she hadn't seen him even once in the last few days. He was the only professor who hadn't made any appearance at McIlwain on the night of Florence's party.

"Miss Falls!" he said. "I'm truly glad to see you!"

Agent Goodman stopped and came back to the doorway of the office. "Do you have permission to be up here, sir?"

"Permission, sir?" he asked. "And who would care to know?"

"Agent Goodman," said Virginia, "this is Dr. Howard Molliby. He's a professor in our department."

Goodman nodded. Dr. Molliby looked interested, suddenly, and gave a nod back, almost a bow. "I'm not here by anyone's permission. A detective named Deacon, of all things, has arranged a sort of rendezvous by mandate."

"Where is Deacon?" asked Goodman. "Do you know?" He tipped forward on his toes, tightening his jaw, looking down through slit eyes at Dr. Molliby.

"Hanging around the attic, according to a policeman I just met on the third floor. Actually, I've been looking for him. We were supposed to meet a half-hour ago. In the department. But as you see, the room is empty."

Goodman stepped aside. "Go on, Professor, lead me to the attic."

Dr. Molliby blew his nose, stuffed his tissues into his pocket, and then led them to the east wing. To their right as they left the seminar room stood a narrow door, half-open. Virginia had seen this door before, but she'd assumed it was a closet or a faculty bathroom. A naked light bulb swung over their heads as they went into the attic, making the wide room rock. The motion made Virginia sick. She closed her eyes to get her balance, then opened them again and saw shadows stretching out, dust swirling in the light over her head, and Deacon holding a flashlight to a wooden beam about ten feet away. A policeman nearby put up his hand and stopped the bulb from swinging. "Sorry," he said. "I ran into it. Too tall, I guess."

"Deacon," said Agent Goodman as he accidentally batted the bulb with his own head. The room swung again. "You got my message."

"Come in," said Deacon. His voice sounded wire thin and tense over Goodman's. He handed his flashlight to one of the five police officers who stood around looking bored. "Goodman," he said quietly, barely looking at Virginia or Dr. Molliby. "Goodman, Goodman, Goodman. Look around at this place. Can you believe it?"

All over the wide, low-beamed room, trailing around the pine plank floor and the pillars that shot up from fiber-glass swamps in distant corners—swirling above the heads of the policemen like cartoon conversation—were whispered words and promises: "I love Susan," "I will love John forever," "Joseph takes Pamela in marriage," "The love of my Emily is prized beyond diamonds and rubies. . . ." And there were dates. 1846, 1866, 1892, 1902, 1954, 1980 . . .

Deacon lit a cigarette on one side of his mouth. He whistled out the other side—a nice trick. "Must be the make-out spot of choice," he said. "We did it in cars, they do it in cobwebs."

"Excuse me, Detective," said Dr. Molliby, stepping forward. "I'm Howard Molliby. I'm sorry I'm a bit late. Actually, I've been looking all over the building for you."

"Glad you found me, Professor," said Deacon curtly. He glanced past him at Goodman and then at Virginia. "Miss Falls, Goodman here called and said your friend got into a fight up in this attic."

She nodded, still feeling a little sick, and nervous, too, as if she were being watched. "He said it happened in the room under the bell tower. He thought maybe it was the same man I saw last night. The man was big, and he kept shouting, 'Where's the ladder? Where's the ladder?'" She paused. "He shouted something at me, too. I can't remember. I wish I could." She shook her head.

"And how's Mr. Falls now?" asked Deacon.

"Mr. *Holc.* I think he might have a concussion."

"We'll go on up to the bell tower. By the way, guess you and Professor Molliby know Agent Goodman by now. He's on loan from the FBI."

Goodman blinked. "Detective, you might want to put out that cigarette."

Deacon shrugged his shoulders, smiled sardonically, and dropped the cigarette to the floor. "Gracious!" said Dr. Molliby, who apparently hadn't noticed it. "We don't want any more fires up here!"

"Miss Falls?" Deacon stamped his cigarette flat and gestured for her and Goodman to follow him across the attic. A door sat at the top of three tall steps. Goodman ducked as he went through it.

Dr. Molliby sneezed behind them. "I'll wait outside for you, Detective."

"Stick with us for a few minutes, Professor," said Deacon. "We may need your McIlwain expertise."

"Oh, but I have no expertise in this portion

of McIlwain. My wife and I came once when we were young and sportive, but I don't do well in attics, Detective. I'm allergic to fiber-glass insulation, among so many other things. No, we didn't linger long in *this* garden of romance, I assure you." He sneezed again.

"Wrap a handkerchief around your face," said Deacon.

"Who carries such things nowadays, Detective?"

"I have one," said Goodman. He pulled a neat handkerchief out of his pocket, and Dr. Molliby took it hesitantly, then held it over his nose.

"A federal agent is always prepared," said Deacon with a smile. He took his flashlight back and carried it in front of them as they entered the next level of attic.

After crossing a plank floor and then climbing another short flight of steps, they entered a wide, floorless room without any overhead bulbs at all. A wooden bridge spanned the insulation, and they bounced over it, knocking the planks with the toes of their shoes.

Deacon's light swung up and down over beams, rafters, planks, and everywhere it landed, words danced: "Frank takes Mary 1892," "I give her my crown—Richard, 1903," "One in marriage, one in missionary service, Ben and Audrey, 1948." Virginia walked at the back of the line, just behind Dr. Molliby, who followed Goodman. She imagined the writers of those words: turn-of-the-century boys in tight collars, lean young men of the 1930s, 1950s football players in crewcuts and tennis shoes, bell-bottomed hippies. They had scaled these splintered beams with their fiancées looking on, yelling out what to write.

"Dr. Molliby," called out Deacon, "where were you last night? The night of the party?"

"I was at home," he called back, his voice muffled by Goodman's handkerchief. "I never received an *invitation*, you see."

"Why should you of all people not have received an invitation?" said Deacon. "You and Mrs. Treadwell went way back, correct? You've known each other as long as she and Professor Katharde."

"Certainly, at least as long. I used to court Florence Treadwell—well, I tried to court her, anyway—before she married. And I have wondered every minute since I heard the news, why on earth would Florence not invite me to an office party? I've suggested such a party year after year. She knows how I long for a little more conviviality around these stodgy halls."

Virginia could barely see Dr. Molliby ahead of her on the bridge, tugging at his Tutankhamen beard.

"But," he said, pausing to sneeze, "I expect that something went wrong with the postal system. Another event-stone in the great pyramid of the universe."

"The what?" asked Deacon. His voice cracked in a laugh.

"I am a pyramidicist." Dr. Molliby made a triangle with his hands in the light Deacon had just turned on him. "I conceive of the world pyramidally. Every occurrence is but a stone in an infinite number of interconnected pyramids. An evil event in one pyramid—that is, Florence Treadwell forgetting to invite an old friend to a Christmas gathering—may be a good event in yet another pyramid—the existence of which I do not as yet comprehend. All events ultimately constitute the structure of the entire universe, which is inherently pyramidical."

Deacon whistled through his front teeth. "What do you make of all that, Agent Goodman? We didn't talk about pyramids in Catholic church."

"I'm no philosopher," said Goodman behind him. "I suppose the professor is trying to discover a divine purpose behind all this."

"The divine *is* purpose," said Dr. Molliby. "That is the point of pyramidicism. God *is* purpose, reason, order, structure, logos."

"So you're saying God is a pyramid?" said Deacon. "Like those pyramids in Egypt, you mean? Where they dig up mummies?"

"There's no need to be so literal about it, Detective."

Deacon laughed.

As they rounded a corner, Goodman's head bumped a low beam, and dust showered down across Dr. Molliby and Virginia. Dr. Molliby suddenly bent into a fit of sneezing.

"You O.K. there, Professor?" Deacon aimed the flashlight back at him. After eight sneezes Dr. Molliby looked up, tears streaming down his face, and whispered hoarsely, "Excuse me, everyone." He bounded back around the corner into the dark, and Virginia heard him sneezing in another room.

"Poor guy," said Deacon.

"Lots of graffiti up here," said Goodman as they passed a beam painted with the words *Luv, luv me Sue, Forever, John.* "How'd all this get started anyway?"

"Actually, there's a tradition at Emmet," said Virginia softly. "Couples go up and ring the bell in three sets of seven to announce an engagement, or seven sets of three to announce a wedding."

The flashlight flitted in another direction.

"Hey!" called another policeman, who also had a flashlight. "Keep your heads down; the door to the next attic is very low."

"The bell tower," said Deacon. "I was up here myself last night. Met some bats. Freezing in here."

Goodman looked up. "Let's go out on the roof and see the bell." He climbed the wooden ladder carefully, stepping gingerly over two rotten steps. At the top he pushed the trap door. "Seems to be locked."

"It wasn't locked when Stephen tried it," said Virginia. "But he tied it shut with his shoelaces."

Deacon snorted.

"If it's only shoelaces we're up against," said

Goodman, "I've got a penknife. Detective, was the door locked when your men checked it yesterday? Hey, it's open. Watch those steps." Icy air rushed down over their faces. One by one they filed out into the December air: Agent Goodman, Deacon, Virginia, and then the handful of policemen with them. All at once they stood four score and three feet above the campus, far far above Glenda Street and the seminary down the hill.

"Kingdoms, castles, guys in black robes." Deacon shuddered and pulled his coat around his chin. His red ears stuck out from his head like stop signs on a bus.

"This place reminds me of that old song," said Goodman with a smile. "*Onward Christian soldiers, marching as to war. With the cross of Jesus going on before. . . .* Right?" He looked at Virginia. "That your school song, by any chance? I used to sing it in church."

"That's not the school song," she said.

"So what is the school song, Miss Falls?" asked Deacon.

She thought for a moment, and then shrugged her shoulders and sang lightly,

> *"Go forth, go forth, dear children,*
> *Salvation in your hand,*
> *This message carry with you*
> *to every distant land—*
> *Though flesh should*
> *fade and perish,*

> *Christ's glory shall shine bright.*
> *Go forth, dear sons of Emmet,*
>   *the purple and the white."*

"Sorry I asked," said Deacon.

"Anyway, it's a nice view," Goodman said as Deacon knelt down to examine a hole in the chicken wire.

"Stephen told me he found a hole," said Virginia. "He climbed out there and went over the rope. Somebody had tied a rope down to the fire escape on the west side."

"No kidding?" said Deacon. He pointed to one of the policemen. "Get a ladder. Send a guy after that rope. I see where the wire was knocked away from the wood here; it's all twisted. I'd say a blunt tool did it, but we'll have to ask the evidence techs. Hey, Agent, you don't even look cold."

"I'm not cold." Goodman frowned. "That's a fairly good drop just down to the roof, then a drop to the fire escape over there, then five stories to the ground. Kind of risky on a slippery roof, too. Maybe Miss Falls's friend did it alone, but I don't believe anybody could have carried a woman out that way, not in this weather. So she left the building another way," said Goodman. "We can assume that."

Deacon leaned against the frame of the bell and took out a notepad. "Mrs. Treadwell was abducted between 7:30 and 8:30. The abductor hit her over the head with the hammer. Maybe the kidnapper took her out early, nearer to 7:30, I mean, by a door on the ground floor. Then he came back to the building later, alone. He left by the attic the second time."

"Three questions," said Goodman. "First of all, where would he have put Mrs. Treadwell in the meantime?"

"Don't know," said Deacon.

"And why would he take such a hard way out?"

"Maybe he was on the run, took the first thing he came to."

"Miss Falls ran into him on the third floor, correct? I can't see an unmarked door on the fifth floor being the first thing he came to."

"Unless he already knew about the attic way," said Virginia, thinking about Raymond Treadwell again. She wanted to tell them, wanted to come in with it.

Both policemen ignored her. "Third question," said Goodman. "Why would the abductor come back to the building at all?"

Deacon pulled the collar of his coat up around his ears. "I think he left something in the building, maybe something valuable or something that might give him away."

"Do you think that's what he came back for again this afternoon?" said Virginia.

"Makes sense," said Deacon. "Don't know yet, though. Don't know much at all yet."

"What else did you find on that hammer?" asked Goodman.

"A little dirt, a strand or two of hair—white,

according to our E.T.'s, probably Mrs. Treadwell's. That's all we have."

"Kidnapping is a frustrating business," said Goodman. "You've got no corpse. Not much evidence, either. Usually you chew your own cud till they ask for ransom, then you give them what they want and hope you can catch them when they're on the run."

They stood shivering against the cold, and then a voice rose from under them, a voice from the grave. "Aren't you people getting cold up there?" A flashlight flickered from the chamber. Virginia saw Dr. Molliby standing below, holding a handkerchief over his nose and mouth.

"Some policeman's calling for you, Detective," he said.

"All right. Let's go," said Deacon. "Everybody down."

The group climbed back into the chamber again and started over the bridge that crossed the upper attic.

"Hey," said Goodman suddenly. "Shine your lights over here!"

Deacon shone the flashlight across the foam floor to a bare spot on the wall.

"Over here, Detective."

"Where?" The light crawled further over the wall till it stopped abruptly on a square of boards straight across from them. Two words loomed large and red in the circle of yellow light. Red streamed down from the letters into the dark.

" 'No Resurrection.' " Deacon read the words aloud. His voice rippled out, and out, and out until it was only a whisper. All around the larger words on the wall were jumbled names from the last century: Aaronsen, Bartz, Spradley, Shade, McIlwain, Melton, Fawcett, Holc. *No Resurrection.*

Deacon swore.

"I want a better look at that," said Goodman. "You get the phone. I'll get some help up here."

A policeman called to them from down below the lower attic. "Deak?" he said. "Deak, are you up there? We've got a message."

"I heard!" shouted Deacon. Heavy footsteps thumped across one of the bridges, further on. "What's the big deal? Who is it? My wife again?"

"No, take a look at this."

A long pause followed. Virginia couldn't see Deacon around the corner, out of the view of flashlights, though she heard him whistle and say, "Well, the old fool!" In a moment, he hurried past her, yelling for the agent. "Come on, Goodman, forget the graffiti. It's Nimitz we're after."

"Dr. Nimitz?" said Virginia, shocked.

"That's right, Miss Falls. You never know where a bouncing check will land."

8

Abelard and Héloise

VIRGINIA PUT HER FACE TO DEACON'S
squad-car window and watched downtown Emmet fly by, restaurants and shops scattering behind them. He directed the driver into a heavily
decorated neighborhood, through tangles of red-
and-green lights, past neat ranks of reindeer and
shepherds. "We're close now," he said. "Slow
down. Closer, closer. There's the house, that little one over on the left."

Goodman sat forward next to her. "There's
another car in the driveway, Miss Falls. Chevy
Chevette. You know that car?"

"That's Dr. Trapp's car."

"Should I hit the siren?" said the driver.

"No!" said Virginia. "You'll scare them half
to death. Please let me come in with you."

"Don't hit the siren," said Deacon. "Miss

Falls—stay in the car. You're only here because I can't spare anyone to take you home." The three men jumped out into the driveway and jogged, hunched over, up to the front door. From the other car, three more followed. Virginia watched the house open and swallow all of them up. Deacon's cell phone lay on the front seat. She reached over, picked it up, and punched in Stephen's number.

"Hello," said a sleepy voice after ten rings. "Hello?" There was a loud *pong*. "Excuse me, dropped the phone. Who is this?"

"Mrs. Holc?"

"Yes?" She sounded sleepy.

"This is Virginia. Has Stephen come home yet?"

"Stephen? Mmmmm, no, I don't think so. I thought he was with you."

Virginia stammered. "No, no, I left him at my apartment. Stephen got in a fight, Mrs. Holc. He's fine, but I think the police took him to the hospital."

"The police? The hospital?" Mrs. Holc paused. "Is he wearing clean underwear?"

"I have no idea! I need you to call Dr. Katharde for me. Tell him the police are about to question Dr. Nimitz."

"Is it that kidnapping business again? I told Stephen—"

"I have to go. I shouldn't even be using this phone. Call Dr. Katharde, O.K.?" Virginia hung up the phone and rolled down her window, exasperated.

"Nimitz!" an angry voice shouted inside the house. "Where's Nimitz?" Upstairs, a woman screamed. Virginia waited a second, then unlocked her door and stepped out.

"Hey!" A policeman stood by the other squad car. "What are you doing?"

"Deacon told me to go in," she said. He started to say something, but she ran up the porch steps and pulled open the storm door.

"Dr. Nimitz?" she called. No one answered. From upstairs came a loud cough and then a moan. "Nooo!" Virginia hurried up the steps. Halfway to the top she heard Lucy Trapp call, "How dare you come crashing in on him. He's sick! Have you got a search warrant?"

"You better believe we have a warrant," said Deacon. He stood in the hall at the top of the steps, looking back and forth between rooms. Virginia started past him into the first open door, the only room with a light on. "Wait," he said, but a group of policemen parted to let her through.

"Lucy?" she said. "Dr. Nimitz?" She turned around in a circle, too conscious of the police at first to find her friends in this mess of a room. Books and papers lined every wall and lay over the floor in piles. "Over there," said a policeman. In the middle of the mess, on a cot, lay Edward Nimitz, as pale as a corpse. Lucy Trapp knelt beside him, wearing her shawl over her head. It looked like the last act of a play.

"Oh," Dr. Nimitz moaned, "I'm dying, I'm dying. Why are you arresting me? I'm innocent."

"You're not dying, sir," said Goodman, who stood at the foot of the cot. "And you're not being arrested. We just want to take you in for a few questions."

"Don't you hear him?" said Lucy Trapp. "What's wrong with you, barging in here like this. My dear, sweet Edward." She leaned over and kissed him on his hollow left cheek, sobbing.

"*Are* you innocent?" said Deacon, suddenly entering the room, his hands in his pockets, his eyes wide open. "Then why didn't you tell the police about the check you cashed yesterday afternoon?" He held up a sheet of paper. "Here's a copy of a check for a thousand dollars: dated yesterday, December 21, and signed by Florence Treadwell. You cashed it at your bank, just before 5:00. It was stopped this morning in Grand Rapids."

"I didn't think of it," said Dr. Nimitz weakly. "I didn't know the check would be halted at the bank."

"You didn't think at all. She's been writing you a check like this every month for the last twenty years. Must be pretty routine by now."

"Detective," Goodman said, "I think we can handle this more calmly."

"You were blackmailing her, weren't you, Professor?"

"No! No!" the old man cried. "I have nothing to do with this!"

"Blackmail! That's ludicrous. This is persecution, the inquisition," said Dr. Trapp. "The inquisition has come to Emmet College."

Dr. Nimitz licked his dry lips. "It isn't what you think it is. I don't know where the money came from, but it only went into scholarships. It was a gift Florence wanted to pass on. She was very private about that. Take me to jail, if it will help save Florence. But I won't betray confidences."

"I want a lawyer for Edward," said Dr. Trapp. "He's not telling you anything else."

"Detective," said Goodman. "Can I see you outside?"

"No," said Deacon.

"Come on, Detective, let's leave them a minute with Miss Falls." He nodded at Virginia as if he expected her to interrogate them.

Deacon shifted back and forth from one foot to the other and finally nodded. The guard went with them, leaving a strange group in the room, two people clinging to each other, and Virginia, clinging to a bookshelf lined with books of theology. She stared around, not quite sure what Agent Goodman expected her to do. Another tall bookshelf rose over Dr. Nimitz's cot, warped from humidity and heat. It looked ready to fall in his direction, ready to send down a gigantic copy of *The Structure of Soteriological Causality* by Howard Molliby.

"I'm sorry, Lucy," said Dr. Nimitz, weakly. "Don't be angry with your poor old Edward."

Dr. Trapp let out a little cry. "I'm not angry with you, darling."

Dr. Nimitz closed his eyes. Lucy sat up, but he lifted his finger and motioned her toward him again. As they put their faces near each other and whispered, Virginia moved backwards toward the door. She went quietly out into the hall, never turning around until she'd shut the door gently behind her. Deacon and Goodman stood at the top of the steps, talking in low tones, their arms crossed.

"This is all wrong," she said. "Dr. Nimitz has nothing to do with Florence's kidnapping. I know who's responsible."

"O.K., so who's responsible?" asked Goodman seriously, and he looked intently at her. She thought of Raymond Treadwell. She had promised not to say anything, but here she was, tempted as all-get-out.

"They taught me back in Sunday school that it's wrong to break a promise," she said, "but I guess I'm about to do it—"

"Sir?" said a policeman just then at the bottom of the steps. "You've got a visitor."

The front door swung open. Virginia looked down and expected to see a policeman, but in came Dr. Katharde. He gripped a folder in his hand, and when he turned his head up, he had that suffering martyr look.

"A woman called me just now," he said, wrinkling up his forehead. "She had a message from you, Miss Falls. She told me I was to come to Edward right away."

Virginia nodded. "Dr. Nimitz is in trouble. You have to tell them everything you told me."

9

Playing Detective

"POOR LITTLE THING, I HAVEN'T FED YOU since yesterday." Virginia closed her front door behind her and bent down to pet Miranda. It was 10:30, but it felt like midnight. She took off her jacket and measured out a cup and a half of Tender Something-or-Others in the kitchen. Miranda knelt down passionately at the bowl, her ears back, her eyes clenched. There was joy in being a cat. Virginia herself had eaten hardly a thing all day, and now she was too tired to eat, much less take joy in it. She took off her clothes and went straight to bed, straight to sleep. She had no dreams. The next morning she woke up to Miranda purring on her head and a voice calling out, "Virginia! Virginia Falls!"

She mumbled, *Speak, Lord, for thy servant heareth.* "In here, Mrs. Viksma!"

A pair of rubber-soled shoes squeaked heavily down the hall. The landlady put her pale face around the door. Her eyes shifted up and down and across the bed. "Dear, are you all right?"

"Fine," said Virginia. She yanked the covers up over her shoulders. "I was just lying here. All by myself, as usual."

Mrs. Viksma's glance dropped to the floor, under the bed. Probably thought she'd see a pair of bare feet sticking out. She came in, broom in hand, and sat down on an old director's chair. She wasn't much smaller sitting than standing. Only the tips of her orthopedic shoes touched the floor. Her gray hair dribbled from the back of a green bandana. "Virginia, we saw you come home last night in a police car, after our bedtime. But Harold said he knew there wasn't a chance in the world that you were in any kind of trouble, you know, of the irresponsible kind."

"No."

"It's not safe around here, Virginia. We've been watching on television about poor Florence Treadwell. I'm sure you knew her, didn't you? I've been trying to think if I ever met her, poor thing. Surely I saw her here and there, but I didn't know it was her, so if I did see her, even if I spoke to her, it couldn't count as a meeting. Of course, I know Milton Katharde a little. He was in Harold's class at the seminary, along with Dick Melton and the Bolthouse brothers and so many other wonderful men of God. We wives had a prayer meeting.

I used to take the boys when they were small—"

"Mrs. Viksma," said Virginia, "you've lived in Emmet for a very long time, haven't you?"

"Oh, yes, except for our years on the field."

"Do you remember the fire in the McIlwain tower?"

She paused a moment and then shook her head. "I was in Africa at the time, but I remember reading about it in a hometown paper someone sent me. Let's see, who was it sent that paper? Thyra. Thyra Perry. She's passed on now. Her son teaches at the grammar school. Do you know Harry Perry, Virginia?"

"No, ma'am."

"Well, that's Thyra Perry's only living relative. Sad isn't it, how people pass away and no one remembers them? But I'll always remember Thyra. She used to go around speaking at those conferences all over the Midwest, talking about male headship in the home. Her husband, Vernon, he would sell her cassette tapes in the back. I wonder if anyone kept copies of those."

"Yes, ma'am."

"And speaking of sons, Virginia—" Mrs. Viksma smiled for a second, and her teeth grew too large and too white. "Do you know who's coming home for Christmas? My two grown sons. Still not married. Handsome boys, you've seen their pictures on my television set."

"Many times." *Too many.*

"And I heard you say you're not planning to go home for Christmas. Why don't you join the

Viksmas? We're one big zoo, this time of year. Right now, you know, we have friends visiting from West Africa." She reached over and patted Virginia's bedpost. "They're really just friends of friends who minister out there, and they've come to the States so the oldest boy can attend Chicago Bible Institute and become a pastor. We're sort of helping where we can. I baby-sit the two younger ones during the day."

"I didn't know you had company now," said Virginia. "I haven't seen an extra car in the driveway."

"They don't have a car. But you must have heard Albert playing the piano. That's the father. How he can play, and I love to sing those hymns. 'Trust and Obey,' 'The Old Rugged Cross,' 'O Zion Haste.'" She started to hum the last one.

"I have seen a couple of little boys around."

"Have you? I've told them to keep quiet and not disturb our little single gal upstairs." Mrs. Viksma winked. It wasn't a casual wink, it appeared to take effort. "Oh my, I think I hear Harold knocking on the ceiling." She hopped up. "Do you hear that?"

"Yes," said Virginia, though she didn't.

"You know how men are. Probably can't find the waffle iron. Hey! Hold your horses down there! I'm coming!"

"Goodbye," Virginia said. She listened for Mrs. Viksma to leave, then got out of bed and ran to the shower. Once dressed, she went straight to Stephen's house. A paper lay untouched on his front steps. Was anyone home? Had something happened overnight, maybe something awful? She had a second of panic. She rang the bell. No answer, so she jiggled the knob of the front door and pushed it gently. "Hello?" she called in a loud whisper as the door swung back all the way to the wall. "Is anyone home?" She took a step in. "Stephen?"

She walked around the corner into the living room, almost stumbling into a tall birdcage containing a large parrot. He screamed at her: "Mozart's in the closet! Mozart's in the closet!"

"Anyone home? . . . Mrs. Holc?"

Across the room, someone whistled. Virginia looked up. There in a corner sat Mrs. Holc. She had headphones on and a small CD player in her lap. She hadn't noticed her guest.

"Hello!" Virginia shouted. An owl hooted somewhere in the house. She took a deep breath. "I said, 'Hey there!'"

"Oh!" Mrs. Holc looked up, startled, and took off the headset. She had Stephen's beaky nose and fair skin. Virginia had met her several times, but never first thing in the morning, without make-up. "I'm sorry," she said. "I was just listening to bird calls. Have you heard the song of the rose-breasted grosbeak?"

"No."

"Ah, but you have! Only *you* thought it was a robin." Mrs. Holc made a warbling noise. "Just remember that one, Virginia, if you ever

137

need a mate. Unfortunately, Stephen's not out of bed yet. The police questioned him half the night. I don't understand why they would question a boy with a concussion half the night, do you?"

"So he did have a concussion?" Virginia sat down on a couch a few feet away.

"Careful where you sit, dear—you never know what you might sit *on*."

Virginia stood up again and brushed off her backside. "Thank you for calling Dr. Katharde last night. I'm sorry I had to leave Stephen to go with the police—"

"You ought to be sorry, Virginia Falls," said Stephen, coming around the corner suddenly. His right eye was a silvery black.

"Stephen—"

"After deserting me last night."

"Virginia," said Mrs. Holc, "for twenty-three years I've fought against all odds to keep this child alive and what does he do yesterday? Flaunts his free will, flies into trouble. Playing detective."

"I'm sorry, Mother," said Stephen. "But I'm not a little boy anymore. I've left the nest."

"You think you're a bird? Birds have more sense than you do. They fly from predators." Mrs. Holc shook back her golden hair. "You're going out, aren't you? You ought to be sleeping."

"Want to join us for breakfast, Mother?"

"I'm going straight to the library. Don't walk, Stephen, you'll wear yourself out in your condition. Borrow the car and take your friend somewhere nice. Tell her to keep you out of trouble."

"Borrow your car?" Stephen said. "You must be feeling generous."

"It's the sight of young love. Makes roses bloom in my heart." Mrs. Holc started to hum as she stood up. "Too bad your father's in Sri Lanka." She smiled slyly and left the room, whistling.

"Stephen," said Virginia, "I really am sorry that I left last night. Anyway, I came to ask you how you're doing."

"Let's discuss our lives over breakfast. I'm starving."

Anita's Pancake Palace sat in the middle of downtown Emmet, across from the city park. They chose a table against the far wall, right under a mural of a woman smiling between stacks of pancakes.

"What do you want to eat?" said Stephen. "My treat."

"I'm not hungry," she said.

"No?" He shook his head and signaled to the waiter. "My friend's not eating," he said, "but *I'll* have what she's having." He pointed to the smiling mural.

"That's one Happy Anita," said the waiter. "Coffee? Orange juice? O.K., back in a minute."

"So," said Stephen to Virginia, "Deacon whisked you from my deathbed last night on police business. That's why you left me, right? And you feel terrible?" He smiled at her eagerly.

"Like I said, I figured they'd take you to the hospital and I'd check on you later, which is what happened. Anyway, you're fine now."

"Oh, tiptop." He put his hand up to his eye.

"Your mother said the police questioned you."

"Yeah. After I saw a doctor, a couple of guys quizzed me for an hour, then Deacon came in late and quizzed me for another hour."

"Tell me what they asked you."

"Boring stuff about the guy I ran into—how much he weighed, how tall he was, what his breath smelled like—"

"Gross." She paused. "What *did* it smell like?"

"Toothpaste. So, who was the guy who came for you in the car last night?"

"Agent Goodman. He's from the FBI. He's helping Deacon."

"What's his first name?"

"I don't know. Why?"

"Just curious. I saw it all from the window of your apartment—I saw this guy sticking his head out, then you getting in his car and leaving me. I hope it's not an indication of the way life will proceed from here on."

Virginia shook her head. "Stephen, they're questioning Dr. Nimitz, but Dr. Katharde knows who really did it."

"Did he tell you?"

"Yes," said Virginia slowly. "Yes, he did. And now he's told them."

"Tell me, then. But wait, here come my

chocolate chip pancakes."

"I'm going to be sick."

He picked up his fork. "Virginia—" He looked around as though he might find someone he knew in the room. "Would you mind saying the blessing?"

"Yes, I would!"

He bowed his head and put down his fork.

She looked around Anita's, tapping her fingers on the table. A waitress glanced over and Virginia waved back. "Stephen," she whispered harshly, "hurry up!"

"Forgive her, Lord," he said. "Amen."

"Stephen!"

While he ate, she repeated Dr. Katharde's long and painful story of the man who had been Florence's husband. "Florence hasn't heard from him once," she said with a final sigh, "in all these years. But she thinks that the mask was a gift from him."

"The mask?" He looked confused for a moment. "Oh, *that* mask."

"Yeah, you remember, Stephen, the one that made an especially tasteless tree ornament. A missionary brought it to her about ten years ago. He said an African had asked him to deliver it. She always thought it came from her husband."

"Why did she think so?"

"Well, it sounds strange, but he thought the mask looked sort of like Raymond Treadwell."

"Maybe we need to find the missionary who brought it and get the whole story from him."

Virginia leaned on her elbows. "Dr. Katharde says it came from Nigeria."

"Nigeria! Lots of missionaries in Nigeria. Could he have said Niger, maybe?"

"I never confuse the names of African countries."

"Just one of the many things I love about you. Let's call MPK and see if he remembers the missionary's name."

"Dr. Katharde had a long talk with the police last night. He told them everything he remembered. They'll follow up on this."

"Come on, do you think the police have time for research into African art?"

She took a sip of water. "Actually, Dr. K. said that the mask had been over at the archives for a while. Wouldn't they have kept an inventory on it? Maybe the artist's name or something?"

"Should we go to the library?"

She thought. "It's closed for the holidays."

"My mother has her own key. She's doing research on the mating habits of vultures in the Peruvian rainforests—hey, what's the matter?"

She had stood up. She was staring out the window of the restaurant. "Stephen, I just saw Lucy Trapp walk by with Dr. Erlichson."

"So. Why are you staring like that?"

"It's just strange. I'll be right back."

"Virginia!"

She hurried out of Anita's Pancake Palace and jogged down the sidewalk. The street was clear. Dr. Trapp and Dr. Erlichson had vanished. After a second of looking around, she walked slowly back. Stephen waited beside his mother's brown Plymouth, his hands on his hips, her jacket over his shoulder. "How could you walk out without a coat? It's like five degrees out here. And you're from Florida."

"I can stand the cold. It gets cold in Florida."

"Yeah, right! Snow on the palm trees!" He laughed. Actually, she was cold, and her jacket was flimsy.

They got in the car, waited for it to warm up again, then eased over icy roads through the neighborhood between the town and the college, zigzagging to the northwest edge of campus. Stephen parked and led them into a tall bank of snow. He shouted up at a dark window, "Hey, Mother! Mother!"

"Throw a rock at the window, Stephen."

"Are you kidding? I couldn't hit the side of a barn with a basketball."

"Here, let me." Virginia plowed back to the parking lot to find a handful of pebbles in the slush. She returned and pitched one, then another, then another, as hard as she could at the window. Each one hit the glass with a *ping*. "My father taught me to throw," she said. "He didn't want me to grow up sissy."

"Oh, thanks a lot."

"I didn't mean anything by that."

Before she could throw another rock, Mrs. Holc appeared at the window, waved, and disappeared again. A moment later she opened a nearby door and shouted to them. They hurried to her. "Mother," Stephen said as they met her in the doorway of a custodial room, "you need to let us into the attic. We're here for research purposes."

"Research? Sure." Mrs. Holc looked down over her bifocals.

"Really. Take Virginia up to Special Collections yourself, if you want to. I'll stay in Reference."

"Hmm. Will she promise not to break anything or write in the rare books?"

"She's an adult, Mother!"

"So are you. Doesn't mean a thing." She touched his black eye gently and clucked her tongue, but motioned for Virginia to follow her. They walked through rows of stacks to an elevator, then rose four stories to the attic where the archives were kept. Virginia looked around at the decor: marble-topped tables, tapestries, silk flowers. In a distant corner stood a suit of armor and in another direction, to her horror, a coffin. Over it hung a picture of a bushy-haired man with a hollow face. Was that man in the box? In the middle of the room rose wooden shelves packed tight with faded books. This was a far more comfortable place than the McIlwain attic, yet an attic was an attic.

"Well," said Mrs. Holc, "what are you looking for, Virginia?"

"A holdings list for the last decade or so."

"An inventory? You want me to help you look?"

Virginia shook her head. "I'll be fine on my own."

Mrs. Holc looked a little sad. "Then I shall go and do the crossword. The *Times* is around here somewhere."

She disappeared. Virginia stepped into the shelves and looked around. On a shelf marked "Various and Sundry," she found a map of Emmet from a hundred years before, then a first edition of Herbert McIlwain's famous antislavery tract "God's Children in the Land of Sorrows."

"Come look at this," called Mrs. Holc after a few minutes. Virginia walked back into the stacks and found her pulling books off the shelf madly. "Have you ever seen these? Works by members of the faculty."

Virginia's eyes traveled over the shelves. She caught sight of a long row of books by Dr. Katharde.

"Fallacies of the Philistines: Why the Academy Can't Conquer the Cross. That's a good one," said Mrs. Holc flatly.

Virginia pulled out another. *"Blind Men's Bluff."*

"That's a bad one," said Mrs. Holc just as flatly.

"What's so bad about it?"

"Blind Men's Bluff? It's not intellectual argument, it's preaching. Sermons in the raw."

"You don't like sermons?"

Mrs. Holc looked shocked. "Does anyone?"

"I used to." Virginia remembered herself on

the front row of that north Florida church, taking furious notes.

"Blind Men in the Buff, that's what my husband called it. It wasn't popular with the Emmet faculty. They all knew he was preaching to *them."*

Virginia smiled and opened the book. She flipped to the middle, to a chapter entitled "A Murder in the Kingdom." She turned a couple of pages and skimmed down to the third paragraph. "Murder!" she read aloud, glancing up at Mrs. Holc, who nodded at her to keep going.

"A Christian scholar does not commit murder! He may scorn his colleagues, ignore his wife, bore his children, pass by the poor, and care little for the mediocre of mind, but he does not murder! He may forget God, neglect the sacraments, covet his neighbor's wife—but he does not murder! A man of letters will not raise the knife, yet his heart is as cold as the heart of a killer!

Christians, let there be no more murder in this kingdom! Our minds must submit to the yoke of peace. Our hearts must bear the whip of love. Our grasp for truth must become a grasp for God. We have set aside visible passions and put away the violence of our bodies. So let us set aside the invisible violence of our minds! Then our King will come again, and rescue His kingdom from this darkness.

"He doesn't beat around the bush, does he?" said Virginia. "Exaggerated use of exclamation points, as always. I think he's probably right, though. After years of innocence I've finally realized that Christians are as awful as everyone else, once you take off the religious mask and look down deep."

Mrs. Holc gave a little sniff-like laugh. "And do you often have the chance to do that, Virginia?"

"No, but I've seen enough. I've seen Christians, including myself, envy, hate, betray, and take revenge—just like everyone else. Only we hide our sins better."

"Or ask forgiveness for them."

"Whatever." Virginia sighed and set Dr. Katharde's book back on the shelf. "I think I'll check on Stephen, make sure he's O.K." She went back downstairs, toward Reference. Stephen leaned out of a row of bookshelves to wave at her.

"Come here," he said. "Look at this."

"Coming."

She found him looking at a stack of blue volumes, each stamped with gold letters: *The Emancipator.*

"Old yearbooks!" She put up her hand to pull 1957 off the shelf. It was nearly out of reach, but she yanked the bottom of the spine and flipped it off the shelf. Stephen caught it and opened it up between them.

"I want to find Raymond Treadwell," she

said. "What are you doing, anyway? Why are you pulling me down to the floor?" She shrugged him off.

"I just thought we'd sit down and look at the book. What's the big deal?"

"I don't like to be grabbed."

"I wasn't grabbing, Virginia. What's wrong with you?"

"Nothing. I'd rather just stand here and look it over by myself. Could you find another one?"

He made a face. "Certainly."

"Good." She looked back down at the yearbook. Stephen walked past her and disappeared into another aisle. Once he'd gone, she sat on the floor and laid the book out flat. Slowly she began to flip through. She came to the faculty pages and saw familiar faces: Dr. Molliby with a black goatee, Dr. Nimitz with hair swirling around his forehead like an anemone, and Dr. Katharde: lean, angular, and sinewy, wearing the same suit Virginia had seen him in many a day (or one just like it?). His face, now simply thin, had once been sharply handsome. His smile in the picture was no more than a thin parting of the lips, a gentle taunt. "Argue with me, argue with me, I am a brilliant young scholar. Argue with me, atheists all. I shall tear you limb from limb."

The next face presented a sharp contrast. It was fat and attentive, smiling at the girl who had placed a trembling finger right over the name underneath:

Raymond Treadwell, prof. biblical apologetics

Virginia grasped the yearbook tightly. "Here he is. Stephen!"

He came around the corner, frowning, and she nearly threw the book at him. "Look! Raymond Treadwell! Can you believe that's Raymond Treadwell?" While he searched for the picture himself, she snatched books off the shelf. 1958, 1959, 1960, 1961. In each volume, there he was, right next to MPK, smiling like a face on a campaign button. Finally, Treadwell's picture disappeared, and Dr. Katharde was left with Nimitz and Molliby, who looked exactly as they did now. Virginia stood up and looked over Stephen's shoulder. He stared at the 1957 Treadwell.

"He looks so familiar," Stephen said. "Where have I seen him before?"

"I don't know."

"Have you seen him before?"

She hesitated, keeping her eyes on the face until it ceased to be a face at all, and she saw only a pattern of light and shadow.

Stephen laughed. "It's like looking for Jesus' face in a tortilla shell."

Just then, there were sharp footsteps on the tile near the reference desk. Mrs. Holc put her head around the stacks. "I thought you'd want to know." She picked a piece of lint from her collar and stared at it. "I stepped out to take a breath of air, and I noticed a huge crowd around McIlwain Hall."

"Is there something going on?" said Stephen.

"I'm not sure, but the police are swarming over campus again. There must be news about the kidnapping. Fly, you foolish little sparrows, fly to McIlwain Hall."

10

Clarity

ON THE CONSERVATORY LAWN, NEW mounds of reporters had sprung up. Camera crews crawled over each other to reach tripods, microphones, hair spray. "Hey!" said a man as Virginia and Stephen passed him, looking for Deacon. He walked quickly after them with a Nikon against his chest, a cigarette in his mouth. "Hey, kids, can I take your picture?"

"Sorry," Virginia said and kept going. Stephen stopped to smile.

"Thanks. Where'd you get that black eye, son?"

Virginia grabbed Stephen around the elbow and pulled him away as hard as she could, past a line of policemen, through a tight circle of reporters, into a loose crowd of spectators. "Let's just find Deacon and ask what's happened.

That's all I care about right now."

He slowed down. "I'm feeling a little woozy, suddenly. Mind if I find a place to sit down?"

"Not at all. But don't talk to anyone."

He turned to the conservatory as she went toward McIlwain. She walked along the rope barrier by the driveway, watching the police, unable to see Deacon or Goodman or anyone from the department. Listening to the chatter from the crowd, she heard *The mask, the mask. What about the mask?* "Excuse me," she said quietly to a pretty woman standing apart from the cameras and vans. "Do you know what's going on?"

"Yes," the woman said in a wispy voice. "A secretary at the college got kidnapped."

"That much I know," Virginia said patiently, "but why are people talking about a mask?"

"A mask was stolen, I think."

"Stolen? Really? When did it happen?"

The woman shook her head, smoothed down her hair, and said, "I don't know anything about anything. My husband probably knows, but he keeps me in the dark about everything."

"Talking behind my back?" A man in a hooded jacket swept up beside her suddenly and kissed her on the cheek, then turned to Virginia with a familiar smile. "Hello there, Miss Falls."

"Why, if it isn't Professor Mark Erlichson. Fancy seeing you here."

"Why? Because I'm supposed to be in Grand Rapids at my uncle's bedside?"

"No, it's not that." She hesitated, unable to say that she'd seen him just a few minutes before with Dr. Trapp.

"Have you met my wife?"

Virginia allowed Mrs. Erlichson to take her hand. Who would have believed it, this beautiful woman with *him?* Even through the wool glove, Virginia felt several large rings. "So," she said to Dr. Erlichson, "did you ever figure out what happened to your keys?"

"Bottom of his sock drawer," said Mrs. Erlichson. "I found them."

"So why did you come back?" Virginia looked intently at Dr. Erlichson. He gave her a mysterious smile behind his beard. There were no crumbs in it at the moment.

"To help out poor Nimitz," he said. "Lucy called me. She said they were giving the old guy a hard time. Milton *would* let the police arrest him without saying a word—"

"You mean 'a word' about Raymond Treadwell?" said Virginia softly.

He blinked twice. "Yes, about that."

"He did tell them all about Treadwell last night."

"Really?" Dr. Erlichson shrugged. "The expurgated version, I'm sure. Nothing about the time Treadwell brought a woman up to Howard Molliby's office after hours—her perfume kept Molliby sneezing for a week. And certainly nothing about Lucy Trapp."

"What about Dr. Trapp?"

"You'll have to ask her yourself."

"Hey!" squealed Mrs. Erlichson, bouncing up to her toes. She pointed to the west door. "Here comes President Avella."

Dr. Erlichson cleared his throat. "Pass out the pillows."

Voices roared all around. The crowd shifted toward the west door as Dr. Avella came toward the reporters, holding a sheet of paper in his hand, nodding his head to let everyone know he was about to speak. Detective Deacon stepped up next to him and held his hands out to quiet the crowd.

"Today is a dark day in the history of Emmet College," said the president, his Adam's apple bobbing like a second chin. "We have now had communication with Mrs. Treadwell's kidnapper, and no doubt remains that we are dealing with a dangerous, demented individual."

Cameras flashed.

"Is it true there's now a ransom note?"

"What about the mask?"

"Is there another suspect?"

"Are the police still holding Edward Nimitz?"

"We need your help," said Dr. Avella in a heavy voice. "Above all, we need your prayers."

"Dr. Avella, do you think that this will affect enrollment?"

"How did the kidnapper manage to get back in the building?"

"The message," Dr. Avella said, "was written—"

"In blood? Is it true that the message was written on a wall in blood?"

"Incorrect. The writing on the wall in the Tower—consisting of the words *No Resurrection*—was put there by means of a painting utensil and red paint. The message that I have received today, delivered on a sheet of plain notebook paper, was typed on an ordinary typewriter. It was left in place of a mask that was stolen this afternoon from the third floor of McIlwain Hall."

His black eyebrows wrinkled up sharply. He held the paper closer to his face. After a pause, he read the note.

"No atonement without sacrifice.
No forgiveness without shedding of
  blood.
Give me a death, and I give you a
  resurrection."

The crowd hushed for a moment. The wind blew, flapping the flag on the Tower, whistling in the dead treetops.

Dr. Avella held the paper closer to his face. "And then," he said, "the note ends with a rhyme:

"Search for her you search in vain,
She's buried under McIlwain."

Virginia suddenly felt dizzy. She looked around

for Stephen and found him on the steps of the conservatory porch, sitting with his head in his hands. She walked toward him, her boots sinking in the mush of trampled snow.

"I feel terrible," he said.

"Yeah, well, you're not the only one."

"My vision's cloudy. You mind driving me home?"

"Let's get out of here." She helped him up, and together they started back to the chapel parking lot. Agent Goodman passed them on the way.

"Hey, have you two you seen Dr. Erlichson?"

Virginia pointed back to the crowd. "He was here a minute ago, with his wife."

Goodman held out his card. "If you see Erlichson, tell him to come talk to me. Mrs. Treadwell's keys, we've identified all of them now. One actually goes to the attic door and the other to the padlock on the door to the Tower. Those must be old keys—no record of them anywhere."

Goodman hurried away. Virginia and Stephen continued to the car, saying little. She couldn't get those words out of her mind: *Buried under McIlwain.* Was Florence already dead? As for Stephen, who knew what he was thinking? He dropped his head back and stared at the ceiling of the car as she drove him home. Finally, at the intersection with the railroad path, he straightened up and said, "Virginia, let's go for a walk."

"I thought you were sick."

"I need air."

They parked the car and headed down the railroad path toward the marsh just west of town. A mile down the path, the white sky touched the ground on every side. Brown stems of old goldenrod still clotted the slats of the icy bridge. The snow on the other bank was clean.

"Look," said Stephen. "I'll have to tell my mother we saw that." Sheets of starlings blackened the sky in the distance behind them. They hung over a lone weeping willow and then fell into it, sheet upon sheet, layer upon layer.

"Stephen," said Virginia, "I keep thinking about Raymond Treadwell, wondering if he's really back, if he's still trying to take revenge because his son died."

"Revenge on whom?"

"On everyone, I guess. He'd turned against everyone. That's why he tried to burn down McIlwain."

Stephen frowned. "I find it hard to believe that a person could stay angry for so long. But you never know. You just never know what's going on inside anyone else."

"I can't imagine," said Virginia, "how a good man can turn so bad. In those yearbook photographs, Raymond Treadwell looked normal, happy."

"He lost his faith."

Virginia shrugged. "A lot of people do. They don't all, you know—"

"Yes?"

"Don't all go off the deep end. They don't all go around setting things on fire, attacking their friends."

Stephen shook his head. "The stronger the belief, the harder the fall."

"I don't understand the passion, then, that precedes a fall like that. I guess you'd say religion never meant that much to me."

"The way I see it," he said, "what you've had with God isn't a divorce, it's an annulment."

"An annulment."

"Raymond Treadwell got divorced from God. It was this intense thing, then it kind of, you know, dried up, and now he's bitter. He's like those husbands who go around persecuting their ex-wives. . . ."

"Letting air out of their tires and torturing their pets," said Virginia.

"Right. In your case, you never had the love affair, you never had the passion, you just had an arrangement of convenience and now you've had an annulment. That's why you don't feel too bad about it."

She thought for a moment. "God and I were never married. That's what you're saying."

"Right."

"Religiously speaking, I'm still a virgin."

"Yep. I won't ask about other categories."

"I should hope not. And what about God? Is he angry at me?"

"Ask him yourself."

"Next time I see him, I will."

They walked on a little further, then turned back, found the car again, and drove home. At the Viksmas she stepped out and handed Stephen the keys. Did she see a face at a downstairs window?

"Get some rest," she said. "Sleep off that headache."

He was looking at the window, too. "I'd shock your landlords if I kissed you right here."

"When you put it like that—" She leaned over and gave him a sisterly kiss, then ran up the steps to her apartment and slammed the door behind her. Two glass coasters rattled on her coffee table.

"Virginia?" came a muffled cry before she'd even sat down.

"Uh-oh."

"Virginia Falls?"

She looked out the window. There was no one outside. Then came a *boom boom boom* on the floor, like someone pounding the ceiling downstairs with a broom handle. She didn't tap back.

Boom boom boom. Virginia put her ear to the floor, and she heard Mrs. Viksma's clear voice: "Virginia! I know you're up there! Please come down!"

"Why?" Virginia asked weakly. She knew she couldn't be heard. She didn't want to go down.

"Help me, please, Virginia. Come quick."

With a groan Virginia picked up her coat again and went back down the steps. She knocked lightly on the Viksmas' front door, trying to see through the porch window. "The door's locked!" she called.

"There's a key in the mailbox! You'll have to open it yourself."

She took out a small key, unlocked the Viksmas' door, and walked into an empty living room. "Mrs. Viksma? Are you O.K.?"

"I'm back here in the master bedroom. Can you help me?"

Virginia went down the hall, past the living room where a trash can made from the foot of a real, live, dead elephant stood at sad attention beside a cluttered desk. She held her breath and looked around the hall floor for a fallen woman.

"Right here, dear, beside the bathroom. Come in."

She turned onto another small hallway, which ended in a large bath and bedroom. And there Mrs. Viksma sat, A-OK, on a king-size bed, next to a small boy with a thermometer in his mouth. A short, thick broom lay on the floor next to a night table. A television flashed soundlessly in the corner: scenes of McIlwain Hall, President Avella, Deacon, and Goodman.

Virginia came further in. The little boy looked up with eyes that sank into his face like black stones.

"This is David," said Mrs. Viksma. "He's very sick. I'm worried because I can't get in touch with his father. I've tried to keep him warm, and

I've given him those things they say to give children nowadays—" She waved her hand at a counter full of red-and-orange liquid medicines. "But I really should take him to the doctor. I'd like Albert to know."

"Where is Albert?" asked Virginia.

"He took my car to Chicago. He's setting up an apartment for Arthur, that's his oldest son. Arthur, as I told you, is attending Bible college in the city, and he doesn't have a phone yet."

"Do you want me to find someone to take, um—"

"David?"

"Yes, to the doctor?" asked Virginia. She imagined herself carrying the child a mile in the snow, fainting in the doorway of the Emmet Medical Clinic.

"Oh, that's no problem," said Mrs. Viksma. "Harold should be home soon with the truck. Do you think—is there any chance you could take a trip into the city for me, Virginia, and ask Albert to come home?"

Virginia opened her eyes wide. "You want me to go to Chicago?"

"I thought you could go with that nice boyfriend of yours—"

"He's not a boyfriend. And he has a concussion."

"Oh well, I guess it's not convenient. Poor little David, without a mother *or* a father."

"All right. I'll go," said Virginia quickly.

"You will? Thank you, dear, thank you.

David, can you tell Miss Falls thank you?"

The boy coughed and nodded.

"Poor thing," said Mrs. Viksma. "In confidence I'll tell you—" she backed Virginia into the doorway and whispered—"he got this fever because he was allowed to run around in the *night air* on Wednesday while his *father* took my Harold's place in that play at the college chapel. Harold had a terrible cold—coughing and sneezing everywhere, so Albert volunteered to sing for him in the chorus. I told Albert not to take the children out with him. They're not used to our climate. But he wouldn't listen to me, brought them home chilled to the bone, and the very next day poor David had fever."

"What's the address?" asked Virginia as she stepped away from Mrs. Viksma into the hall.

"It breaks my heart to think about. They have no other family in the world to help them, just some friend or other in Michigan, not to mention Harold and I. Harold and I, we knew Albert's pastor in Africa. He's the one who contacted us about helping him. And it's not that we haven't done everything we can. . . ."

"No, ma'am. If I'm going to catch the next train—"

"Albert's not a practical man, but he's highly intelligent. He plays that piano and does his art most of the time—see that statue he made of Harold?" Virginia's eyes followed Mrs. Viksma's finger to a hunk of clay on a table in one corner. It did look a lot like Harold Viksma.

Mrs. Viksma scribbled something on a piece of paper from her apron pocket and pressed it into Virginia's hand. "Here, you'll need the address, dear. Now, take care."

Virginia grabbed the paper and hurried on to the station. One train had just left. The next was due in forty-five minutes. She sat alone and waited, looking through the large, warped windows of the station into the woods on the other side. Birch and hawthorn and willow rippled up on the distorted glass, then dissolved in gray lines before bubbling into mushrooms of green and blue. When the train finally came, it spilled across the windows like a river of green water.

The car she climbed into was thick with cigarette smoke. Newspapers stood up in rows, lilies in bloom. How could these people read without getting motion sick? She sighed and looked out the window next to her. This window, at least, was clean and unwarped. The roads outside were straight, stretching as far into the horizon as the eye could see. If there was one thing she appreciated, it was clarity, and the Midwest was full of it. She remembered a conversation with her mother, six years ago.

"Can't you find some school in the South?" her mother had said pitifully. "With you gone, I'll be all by myself in the house here." She had meant, "All by myself with your father."

"I want to live where it's cold," Virginia had answered. She probably could have thought of something better to say, but her father sat there in his usual chair, listening, or maybe not listening, and she wanted to pitch a reason out, hard, that sounded absolutely unimportant.

"Honey, there are cold places nearer to home," her mother tried again. "Why not that Christian college in Kentucky you told us about? It's Methodist, like you are, and they have snow in Kentucky."

"Mama, haven't you heard what I've been saying? Emmet's giving me a scholarship. I won a full scholarship to college. I thought you'd be happy. You all don't have to pay one single cent for my college education."

"Let her go," that ugly voice had declared from across the room, the voice that always made her mother jump. "You heard what she says. She doesn't need her family. All she needs is God. She doesn't need her mama. She's big hot stuff now, and she's ready to live with a bunch of Yankees, so let her."

Thinking about her father always gave her a gray feeling.

When she stepped out of the train into a neighborhood of chain fences and pale tenements, the heavy clouds lay puckered on the building tops. It was an eight-block walk: long, Chicago city blocks. Could she get back before dark? It didn't matter. She wasn't afraid.

The wind swept up trash from the street and lifted it over her head. The streets crisscrossed at perfect intervals like lines on a grid, segmented by sidewalk cracks. Each crack marked

Virginia's journey further into the drab, into the pale geometry of the city. Because of the cold, few people loitered on the street or sidewalks. A couple of children played on swings outside a building with wax-paper windows. Low-riding cars pounded by. They disappeared on the horizon, at that point in infinity where the streets met.

She reached the dirty yellow high-rise. Inside was a ramshackle lobby and a curving staircase. She climbed to the landing of the eighth floor, following the address. The stairs ended here. All the bulbs were out. The only light came from a gash in the ceiling.

"Hello?" someone said behind her on the steps. She held her breath. A man came around the curl of the steps in the half-dark. He stopped about seven steps back. She strained to see him but didn't move.

"Are you lost?" he said.

"I'm looking for somebody."

"Who are you looking for?"

"An African man. I was supposed to bring him a message."

"What's his name?"

"If I can go back down in the light, I can look again at the address I brought with me."

The man turned, and she followed him two flights down. He was black and slender, wearing a thin pink shirt that shimmered over his bony shoulders. Once in the light, she realized that he was only a boy, maybe seventeen or eighteen. He bent low over the address Mrs. Viksma had given her.

"I think it says not 823 but 523. We have to go one floor down, do you think?" His accent was foreign—high and sharp, but pleasant.

"Yes, that's fine."

On the next landing down, he swung the door open for her. It wasn't locked, or even latched. The hall smelled like a park toilet. It had no windows or bulbs, but rods of pale light shone at the bottom of each door. She heard voices on the other sides of the doors: scratch, scratch, scratching. Steel-wool voices.

"Here it is. 523." He smiled.

Virginia held her knuckles up. "Guess I'll knock."

"Maybe I have a better idea." Still smiling, he pulled out a key and put it in the lock. The door swung open and flapped against a hinge.

Virginia faced him, startled. He had tricked her into coming to his apartment. She stepped back, about to start running.

"It's O.K., it's O.K." He smiled. "Come in, please. Did I surprise you? I am Arthur Amalya. Albert Amalya is my father. He isn't here right now, but I hope he'll come back this evening. Would you like to wait for him?"

Virginia came in slowly and looked around. She saw no place to sit, no chairs or table. The cold air was thick with dust. "The reason I came," she said, "is to tell your father that your brother David is sick."

Arthur Amalya's smile disappeared. He took the paper Virginia had been holding and stared at it, as if it would tell him something she hadn't. "Very sick?"

"Mrs. Viksma thinks so. Where is your father? Could we reach him?"

Arthur scratched his head. "My father went to Michigan. Maybe when he comes back—no, I better go myself."

Virginia looked around anxiously, not wanting to meet Arthur's eyes for more than a few seconds at a time, but not wanting to sink alone into the dirty gloom of the room. "I came on the train," she said. "It's a long walk from here to the station."

He nodded soberly. "I'll leave my father a note and go with you. Let me get my jacket, all right?"

"Yes, fine," she said.

While he went to the back of the apartment, she walked further in to see the view from the main window. She looked down on the ragged street below, on dark figures moving back and forth. Was that a child there in the middle of the road? She stepped forward to see further down and bumped into a small stack of boxes under the windowsill. The box on the top fell over on its side, half-open.

The child in the road made it across safely. Virginia relaxed and watched for a moment, then picked up the box she'd knocked over. Without thinking, she lifted the lid. A wooden face grinned back at her.

Arthur came around the corner just as she closed the box and stood up again, her mouth wide open.

"All right," he said. "Ready to go?"

"Yes." She was shaking. "There's a mask in there," she said, pointing at the box.

"Yes," he said nonchalantly.

"Where did it come from?"

"Africa. My father made it. It's a hobby of his, woodwork, sculpture." Arthur cleared his throat. "I'm ready to go."

She stood up weakly and followed him out of the apartment, down the sharp-smelling hall to the stairs. The mask had come from McIlwain Hall, no doubt about it.

"Arthur," she said quietly, calmly, though she wanted to *shake* the truth out of him. "How long have you been in the United States?"

"A few months."

"But you speak English so well. Like an American."

"My father is an American." They hurried down the last few flights of stairs. As they left the building, they passed by a group of boys twined around the main door, smoking something. Arthur smiled at them, nodded his head, and said, "Believe in Jesus."

The boys laughed. The sky had turned navy. An old lady with an oily-looking bag watched them pass, then followed slowly for a few steps before she turned away.

"Tell me more about your father," said Virginia, trying to keep her voice even. "Where is he from?"

"From here," said Arthur. "He used to be a teacher here in Chicago, before he went to Nigeria to teach and met my mother. She was a student of his."

"But you have no other family in the United States."

"No. Not that I'm aware of."

"Not that you're aware of," she repeated.

They walked the rest of the way quickly, in silence, and arrived outside the train station at dark. It was snowing. Windy snow lassoed their shoulders. No one else waited with them, but Virginia checked her watch and figured the train was due to arrive any minute.

"You came a long way to find me," Arthur shouted just as the train lights edged around a curve in the distance and the tracks moaned eagerly. "I hope I can return the favor sometime." She looked at his innocent face and nodded her head. He nodded back. The wind rose up around their feet. They stepped on the train together and headed back to Emmet.

11

Car Chase

ALL THE WAY HOME, VIRGINIA WAS
quiet. Arthur sat next to her, talking about his
plans for seminary, a pastorate, then the mission
field. He wanted to go back to Africa, he said,
where people really needed him. "I would like
to begin a school. And I would name it after
my father, because he has taught me everything." While he talked, he shook his hands in
the air, and his reflections in the green windows
on both sides of the aisle joined him like a small
congregation. She nodded, half-listening, half-
dreaming as she stared at the dark outside. In
her half-dream she saw the mask. She saw a
faceless man rumbling toward her from a black
doorway, charging over spears of broken glass.
Was it Arthur's father?

They left the train at Emmet and walked

together back to the Viksmas. "Would you like to come in?" he said when they reached the house.

"I have some things to do. But maybe I'll see you another time." She shook his hand nervously.

He nodded. "Goodbye."

"Goodbye, Arthur. Good luck." She watched him go in and then ran upstairs and dialed Stephen's number.

"Stephen, it's me. I need your help."

"Where have you been for the last five hours? I've been calling."

"Does your mother have a key to Fawcett Chapel?"

"My father keeps one around."

"Meet me there as soon as you can. I'll call the police, too. I need to talk to them, but I don't want them coming up to my apartment."

It took her less than fifteen minutes to walk to the chapel. She waited under an awning at the back until Stephen came jogging down the street, bouncing against the whirl of snow. "Got the key," he said, "but I couldn't borrow the car."

She shivered. "Just hurry."

He jiggled the doorknob. It opened without a key, and he laughed back at her. "Stood out here in the cold all the time, did you? Didn't even try the door just to be sure?" It was almost as cold inside the chapel as out.

"So what's going on?" he said as she turned a light on and took off her scarf.

"Let's go into the auditorium, and I'll tell you about it."

The main floor of the auditorium was not on ground level but up a flight of steps. They climbed the steps and tried the side doors but found them locked.

"Probably locked Wednesday night," Stephen said, "to keep kids from walking in and out, interrupting the play." The backstage door was around a corner. Stephen opened it, and Virginia stepped in beside him to switch on lights. They both took a breath as bold yellow flooded the darkness.

"Come here," said Virginia, and she pulled Stephen in. Shining curtains hung above them. A few feet away in the wide glaze of the stage sat an empty crèche. A foil star glittered over the frame of a stable next to it. Behind the scene, risers fanned up under painted green sheets, a pair of terraced hillsides. Virginia imagined Albert Amalya hovering there two nights before, waiting for his time to come. "I found the mask this afternoon, Stephen."

"The mask?" He had sat down at the piano on stage. He jerked his head up. "Where was it?"

She told him about her trip to Chicago, about Arthur Amalya and his father. "I saw the mask in Arthur's apartment. He says his father carved it."

"So why would Amalya come back to steal his own mask?"

"I'm not sure he did steal it. According to Arthur, he's been in Michigan today."

"Do you think Arthur stole it, then?"

"No." She thought of him preaching to the train window. "He wouldn't do that."

"Somebody stole it, Virginia. Don't take anybody's innocence for granted." Stephen looked absent-mindedly down into the auditorium. "For instance—hey!" He jumped up to his feet. "Hey, who's out there? Stop!"

Across the auditorium someone started to run. There was a screech and a bump down in the seats.

"Virginia," Stephen said, "find the main lights!" He jumped over the stage light onto the floor level and ran out of sight, into the blackness.

"Stephen?" Virginia dived for the side of the stage and looked for light switches. *Which switch?* She tried one after another; lights flashed on and off around stage, in the hall.

Stephen yelled again. "Where are the lights?"

Virginia had tried all the switches. She heard a thud, a grunt, and a loud volley of footsteps. She hesitated, leaning toward the door, then ran back across the stage and jumped down to the auditorium floor. "I'm coming"

She had no idea what she might do next. The steps from the balcony curved down to the side aisles. She ran for the staircase on her left, plunging through a row of wooden folding chairs, snapping them up with the tips of her fingers until she reached the stairs. She raced up to the balcony. Under a big row of arched windows, she paused.

The two men were exactly below her, wrestling in the dark. She heard Stephen panting. She saw the white hood of his jacket. He fell back. The other man was just underneath her; she heard the low thrum of his voice. "Don't try to get up, or I'll kick you in the mouth."

On the rail next to her sat a tall stack of hymnals. She gave them a shove and felt a sudden cloud of wind in her face. "Look out, Stephen!"

The hymnals boomed as they hit wood. The man yelled. She stared down into the shadows, watching a big figure stand, reel, sway, and fall headlong.

"Stay where you are!" commanded someone from the stage. All sound stopped as if the whole room had just plunged underwater.

Virginia put her hands up to her ears. A policeman stood in the lights, shining a golden beam in her direction. He jumped from the stage, and the main lights flickered on as his shoes hit the floor soundlessly. "Agent?" he called.

"Right here." Agent Goodman stepped out from under the balcony and looked up at Virginia. He glanced down at the white man, who lay face down in the aisle, arms stretched out flat, a dress shirt hiked up around his stomach.

"Miss Falls," said Agent Goodman. "Come downstairs, please."

She stared out at the stage, dazed. The foil star shone back at her.

"Miss Falls," said Goodman again, "downstairs, please?" He knelt over the injured man. Virginia heard footsteps behind her. She felt a hand on her arm and turned. It was the policeman. She recognized him as one of Deacon's drivers.

"Take it easy," he said. "Come on downstairs. Everything's fine."

She followed him, clinging to the stair rail.

"Everything's O.K.," he said, then shouted, "Hey, Agent, that guy dead down there or what?"

"No," Goodman called back calmly. "Better call an ambulance, though."

As Virginia came in under the balcony, Stephen was just lifting himself into a wooden chair. Goodman studied him coolly. "This guy assault you, son? Is that what happened?"

"No, sir."

"Did you assault him, then?"

"Yes, sir."

"With what purpose in mind, may I ask?"

"Well, he ran. I guess I chased him down. I figured he was up to something or he wouldn't have run."

"Interesting logic." Goodman checked the man's breathing and pulse again, then sighed and looked up to the balcony. He looked down at the hymnals, then over his shoulder at the stage, and finally he leaned forward, his forehead touching his knee. "One of you did call the police, correct?"

"Yes, sir," said Virginia. "I left a message for

Deacon, earlier. I've got something I'd like to discuss with him—and you."

"All right."

Just then the body moved. "Ahnnn," the man groaned. He lifted his head slightly from the floor, and his arms drew in. In one swift motion he rolled over and dropped his hands to the floor again. "Oh, my, where am I?" He was an older man, about sixty, large and darkly freckled above his gray beard. His long hair closed back in a ponytail.

"What's your name, man?" said the policeman.

"I'm a custodian. Someone knocked me down." The big man closed his eyes, and his head lolled to the side.

Goodman flipped out a badge. "I'm FBI Agent Goodman, sir. Do you have any ID?"

"I don't have any with me—well, I have a temporary driver's license." He took a crumpled paper from his pocket and handed it to Goodman. "I haven't done anything wrong. I work for the college. I came back tonight to clean up the stage. We didn't have a chance on Wednesday night."

"You're not in trouble," said Goodman. He glanced at the ID and put it in his pocket. "I'm just bound to ask you a few questions. You were planning to clean up in those clothes?"

The man bent forward and looked at his dress shirt and pants. He seemed confused.

"Miss Falls," said Goodman, "may I see you

for a second?" He motioned to Virginia, and they stepped around a doorway into the narthex.

"This is all a big mistake," she said before he could get a word out. "We heard someone run and then Stephen panicked, then I panicked, then it just happened."

Goodman nodded, narrowing his eyes.

She put her hands over her face. "I shouldn't have come here. I'm so sorry."

"Why did you call the police, Miss Falls?"

"Because—" She opened her fingers to look at him. Her tongue felt like a rock in her mouth. She stumbled over it. "Because I saw the mask. I know where it is."

Goodman watched her. "The mask? So where is it?"

"It's in Chicago. I can give you the address." She took out the note Mrs. Viksma had written and handed it to him.

"Who lives at this address, Miss Falls?"

"Arthur Amalya," she said. She noticed a change in Goodman's expression. "He says his father made the mask—What, why are you making that face?"

"What was the father's name?" asked Goodman. He took a step toward the door, holding up the address Virginia had given him.

"Um, Albert," she said.

"Uh-huh." He pivoted lightly and stepped back toward the auditorium.

"Wait." She followed him back into the auditorium, where Stephen sat rubbing his temples.

The policeman stood nearby, his hands on his hips. The custodian was nowhere in sight.

"Where is he?" Goodman asked quickly but quietly.

"That janitor?" said the policeman. "I let the poor guy go to the rest room. Said he felt sick to his stomach."

Goodman jogged down the nave of the chapel, turned a corner, and bore down suddenly on a side door. It skipped back and ricocheted against his shoulder, then slammed behind him. The policeman looked up, surprised, and followed.

"What is it?" said Stephen. "What's going on?"

Virginia stood dead still. "I don't know."

"Well, come on. Let's go out the front way, maybe we'll catch him."

Somewhere down another hall an outside door creaked open and slammed shut. Virginia followed Stephen under the balcony, through the narthex, and out the front doors of the chapel. The sidewalk was empty. Deborah Street flowed calmly by, just a thin gray ribbon in the evening snow. Around the corner, though, back toward McIlwain, a voice broke the quiet: "Freeze!" There was a screech and a *whiz,* and then a small black car fishtailed across the chapel parking lot and spun onto the new snow of the street. It was the Viksmas' car. It backfired as it recovered itself, and a return shot echoed from McIlwain.

"They're shooting! Get down!" Virginia

didn't know if she'd yelled it, or Stephen. She bent her knees and slid down against the brick wall of the chapel. He squatted and looked around the corner. A police car flew past them. It hit its siren just as it thunked onto the street and took off. Another squad car followed, then a third, chewing up the white, tearing through the gray air. Virginia stayed bolted to the wall. Stephen stood up, but she grabbed his arm and pulled him back. "Better stay here."

"Let's find a car and follow them, Ginny."

"Oh, sure, I'll wait here while you steal one, *Stephen.*"

He sighed and stood up against the door of Fawcett Chapel again, on a rubber mat slick with ice. Virginia listened. She heard voices in the parking lot, then in the chapel. After a moment, though, the voices were swallowed up in the slow hiss of car wheels down Deborah Street, coming closer. A silver Volvo pulled up next to the sidewalk, and Dr. Katharde looked out the driver's window, pointing back in the direction of the speeding police cars, about to say something.

"Is something happening?" he called. "We were on our way to speak with the detectives, and we heard the sirens." He leaned back, and Virginia saw Dr. Molliby in the seat next to him, fidgeting with his bow tie.

"They're going after him!" shouted Stephen, starting to run for the car. "Give us a ride."

"Stephen!" said Virginia. She pulled him

back, but he snatched his arm away, beckoning to her to come too. Dr. Molliby leaned over to unlock the back door, and Stephen jumped in. She followed reluctantly.

"Now, what's going on?" Dr. Katharde asked, breathing quickly. "Whom are the police chasing?"

"It's some custodian," said Stephen. "He was running through the chapel, and I knocked him out—"

"Hardly," said Virginia.

"And then the police showed up, and he ran for it."

"A *custodian,*" said Dr. Molliby. "Milton, did you hear that? He's been with us, then, all along—"

"Of course he has, Howard. That's what I've been saying. He can get to us anytime he wants."

"Hurry!" said Stephen.

Dr. Katharde nodded and shifted down, his bare hand white on the gearshift, his jaw tense and jutting forward over the steering wheel. He jogged the Volvo up over a sidewalk and brought it down hard in the slush, pointed the other way. The wheels spun.

A set of police taillights whirled around a corner ahead of them, leaving red streaks in the air. Dr. Katharde revved the engine and followed. The back of the car skipped like a kite on a string, but it kept its hold on the pavement, slowing and digging in with the turn. Heading up to the railroad tracks, Dr. Katharde got a running start. They soared off the ground suddenly, bounding down again just past a stop sign. Virginia curled her hands under her seat belt. Stephen's eyes were wide; he sat straight up on the seat.

A minute more and they were on the expressway, the Volvo bounding over pits in the road. They glided over to the left lane and hugged the concrete ribbon that unraveled along the median. An orange light flashed ahead: CONSTRUCTION 1500 feet.

"We're going to lose him," said Stephen. The police were out of sight; a wide mobile home glided on a trailer in front of them, taking up both lanes. Soon the lanes narrowed to one, and traffic slowed almost to a standstill.

Dr. Molliby put his head against the glove compartment. "This is only one pyramid, Milton," he said. "Only one pyramid in the construct of eternity. We must be calm. God will make a perfect whole of all these imperfect parts."

"Oh, Howard," said Dr. Katharde, "I wish I had your faith in the whole. I don't care to see eternity at the moment. I only want to see Florence."

Outside the concrete barrier, on the shoulder, another police car whizzed by, its siren wailing.

Stephen sighed. "They'll get him. We just missed it, that's all."

They crept slowly forward in the traffic, staring at the sign on the back of the mobile home ahead: Deercrest Homes, Where Luxury Sleeps. None of them spoke. Then suddenly the wide load picked up speed, and they were out on the broad highway again. The concrete barriers broke into orange barrels; the road opened into five lanes.

"Hey, look there!" said Stephen. A cluster of blue lights flashed at the side of the road. Dr. Katharde brought the car quickly over and stopped fifty yards past the police. Dr. Molliby bounced up in his seat, struggling nervously with his door and seat belt. "Dear Lord, help me with this contrary mechanical device." Stephen hopped out and jogged toward the lights.

Dr. Katharde sat still in his seat, watching.

"We're coming!" shouted Dr. Molliby. "Milton, hurry. Oh, this horrible—" Finally the seat belt unlatched and whipped back under the seat. He staggered out of the car and ran, half-skipped, toward the shoulder of the highway.

Virginia got out hesitantly and walked after him, wondering when Dr. Katharde would come. It was all black around her. Ahead of her, against the lights, hunched the silhouette of a small crowd, a huddle of agents and detectives looking down, heads together. Even bending over, Agent Goodman towered over the others. Deacon must have joined the chase along the way; he stood a few feet back from the main circle, talking into his phone. As she came closer, Virginia smelled smoke and saw what he and the other men stared at. It was the bent body of the Viksmas' car. It had wrecked against a light pole, blacking out all the lights on this side of the highway.

"Is anybody alive in there?" asked Stephen, joining the crowd. As Goodman turned to answer, the door of the car opened, and a large man fell onto his knees on the pavement. A policeman jumped forward and handcuffed him.

"Oh my goodness," said Dr. Molliby, gasping. "Oh my goodness, oh my goodness!"

"Albert Amalya," said Goodman, "you are under arrest." Virginia stared at the custodian bent over on the ground: white haired, fair skinned, blue eyed. She couldn't believe what she'd just heard. Albert Amalya, Arthur Amalya's father, a white man? His head dropped to his knees as Goodman read him his rights. Virginia heard someone walk up behind her. It was Dr. Katharde.

"Milton!" said Dr. Molliby.

"I haven't done anything wrong," said Amalya, still looking at the ground.

Goodman was breathing hard. He shook his head. "Why did you run away from us?"

"I can't explain. I needed more time." Amalya lifted his head and locked eyes with Dr. Katharde. Then, at last, the three men moved together in Virginia's mind: the professor in the yearbook, the mask maker, the custodian.

"Milton," said Amalya, "please believe me. I'm a changed man."

Dr. Katharde slowly shook his head. "Welcome back, Raymond."

12

Reunion

TWO HOURS LATER, DR. NIMITZ LEFT
the Emmet Police Station on the arm of Lucy
Trapp. His thin hair fell into his eyes. Lucy patted him on the back with the heel of her hand,
as if she were burping an infant. Virginia
watched them from the glass window of the
jail lobby next door.

Dr. Molliby bounced up from his chair and
stepped next to her to see. *"Gloria deo,"* he
said, taking out a handkerchief. "They'll leave
Edward alone now. At least that's one thing to
rejoice about." He sneezed violently and looked
over his shoulder at Dr. Katharde, who sat on
a hard chair across the room, his head in his
hands, his long legs stretched out. Getting no
answer, Dr. Molliby turned and put his nose
against the glass. A misty circle appeared from

nowhere, a tiny galaxy against the dark. He wiped it off with the handkerchief.

"I wonder what's taking Deacon so long," Virginia said.

Dr. Molliby sighed. "They must have many questions to ask Raymond. I have a few hundred for him, myself. Don't you, Milton?" Again, Dr. Katharde didn't answer.

Virginia crossed her arms. She watched Lucy Trapp, far away now across a parking lot, helping Dr. Nimitz into her car. He bumped his head slightly, fell back, and finally stumbled down into the seat.

"Where is she?" Dr. Molliby said. "That's what I would ask Raymond Treadwell. Where in the universal construct has that miserable apostate hidden our Florence?"

Stephen put a magazine down and stood up, walked over to Virginia, took some change out of his pocket, and counted it on the palm of his left hand. It was quiet in the long lobby, except for a few police officers talking around the desk at the other end.

"You want more coffee, Ginny?"

"Another cup would be lethal." She leaned back against the window. Stephen reached down to take her hand, but she held it away, aware that Dr. Molliby was watching them. A door opened beside the policeman at the desk. A bony young officer signaled to them. "Back this way," he said. "Detectives are waiting to talk to you."

"All of us?" asked Virginia.

"Shhh," said Stephen. "He might say no." Virginia shrugged and glanced behind her as they started forward. Dr. Katharde hesitated, then got up and walked after them. He wiped his eyes. They entered a darker, older hall, that was punctuated by black doors. Virginia stayed close to the others. At the very end of the hall, the officer stopped and knocked loudly on a tall, heavy door. The door opened. Agent Goodman looked out.

"Sorry for the wait," he said. "Come in."

"Where's Raymond?" said Dr. Molliby, blowing his nose.

"Amalya's in the infirmary." Goodman pointed to a door across the hall.

Dr. Molliby stared at it. "The man's *name* is Treadwell," he said. "Whatever ridiculous things he's told you, the name is Raymond Treadwell."

"Come in, Professor. Come in, everyone." Goodman shut the door behind them. "The suspect has a sprained shoulder. He's in some pain. I've questioned him a little, and Deacon's with him now."

"Do you know where he's taken Florence?" asked Dr. Katharde quietly, stooping forward. His forehead nearly touched the agent's.

Goodman scratched his chin and sighed. "Fact is, Professor, we don't know much. And we have very little to hold Amalya on. The kidnapping occurred sometime between 7:30 and 8:30. He claims to have been performing in a Christmas pageant during that hour."

Dr. Katharde groaned. "In the pageant. How could I not have recognized him?"

"Well, what about the mask he took from McIlwain?" said Virginia. "Can't you arrest him for theft?"

"I can't prove he took that mask," said Goodman. "Anyway, it's not Amalya I want right now, it's Mrs. Treadwell. I need him to lead us to her. I'll hold him on suspicion awhile, search his car and his living quarters. Then I may have to let him go and watch him. I'm worried time's running out."

Dr. Katharde looked at the infirmary door. "May I see Raymond, Agent Goodman? I'd like to speak to him alone for a minute."

Goodman frowned. "If you talk to him, I'll have to have a policeman present. And I'll need to view it on the monitor."

"Must you? If it were just the two of us, he might be inclined to tell me more of the truth."

"Hah," said Dr. Molliby. "Raymond doesn't remember what the truth is."

"Those are the rules," said Goodman to Dr. Katharde, and the professor nodded. The two of them went out the door together.

Dr. Molliby clucked his tongue. "Don't be gullible, old friend. Remember how cunning he is. Be as wise as a serpent."

"Pray for me, Howard."

Goodman returned alone a few moments later. He motioned for Stephen, Virginia, and Dr.

Molliby to follow him. Goodman led them into a long room, bare except for a refrigerator and a rickety table. Mounted in one corner was a television. He flicked it on with a remote lying on the tabletop. A hazy green figure appeared on the screen—Albert Amalya, or Raymond Treadwell, or maybe the devil himself—stretched out on a white cot, his arm in a sling, his hair uncombed. His feet, close to the camera, stuck up like donkey ears around his head. Dr. Katharde moved in next to him and sat down.

Virginia felt as though she had her eye to a keyhole. "Does Treadwell know we're watching?"

"Yeah," said Goodman. "He'll be on his guard."

"Raymond," said Dr. Katharde from the television, his voice distant and scratchy, buzzing on the bare walls of the room where they sat, "tell me what you've done with her."

"Milton!" Amalya slapped the metal rail of his cot. He was a huge man, still muscular. "Milton, look at the circles under my eyes. You think I've slept since Wednesday? I don't know where she is. Whatever you think about me—"

"Mendax mendacium," mumbled Dr. Molliby. "Liar of liars!"

"Hush," said Virginia.

"Those are black eyes, Raymond!" said Dr. Katharde. "You've been fighting. And you know exactly where she is." Dr. Katharde's face looked mottled in the strange light. "Raymond, *Raymond,* I plead with you. Tell us."

"I'm not the one who did this. I'm not Raymond Treadwell anymore, either."

"Hah!" said Dr. Molliby.

"You say you're a different man," said Dr. Katharde. "I pray that means you haven't harmed her." His voice rose. "If you need money, you can come to me. But this seems like rage, Raymond. Put it away! Asking for my death accomplishes nothing!"

"When did I ask for your death?" Amalya coughed, or maybe laughed. "That's ridiculous."

Dr. Katharde winced and bit his lower lip as though he were about to cry. "It's my life that you are looking for in exchange for her life. You've hated me. I understand that."

"No."

"It's the *truth!*"

"No, Milton. My sins are behind me. I'm a new man."

"A *new* man?" said Dr. Katharde, leaning forward, almost whispering. "But it was the *old* Raymond Treadwell who was here on Wednesday night. His hand was in this! You and I remember the fire in the Tower so many years ago. Your family might have died there because of your . . . your *thirst* for suffering. How can you ask me to believe you're not the one who did that? You ask me to believe that you're someone else?"

Amalya groaned. He was quiet for a moment,

then rubbed his eyes. "I got justice for what I did, you can be sure of that, Milton. I lost my family. I've been in exile. But I have found peace. Isn't that what God promises us?"

Dr. Katharde leaned down close to Amalya, his hands wrapped around the bed handles, his sharp elbows sticking up on both sides of his back like the arms of a rocking chair.

"I went to Africa," continued Amalya, "and I found an African woman, a pagan pure and simple. I rescued her from a bar in Lagos, and we lived together. She spent every dollar I had. She was the freest woman I ever met, no conscience about anything. She had my children, never asked to marry me. Years went by. I began to get some peace. But this woman, she met missionaries, and she became religious. She died, and I was stuck in grief again." Amalya's mouth went crooked. "Stuck in the dung of this life. No one escapes God, Milton. I repented. I surrendered because I couldn't win against God."

"But why did you try to do battle with the Almighty, Raymond? I lost my wife a few years ago, but *I* didn't hurt anyone, *I* didn't attack anyone. *My* faith never wavered."

Dr. Molliby nodded his head at the television. "These tragedies all make sense when we understand the underlying structure of things. Raymond never could comprehend that. I *tried* to explain my philosophies to him—"

"Listen," said Goodman.

"I don't know where Florence is, Milton, I

promise you!" For the first time, Amalya raised his voice. "I wrote her when I came here," he continued. "She forgave every horrible thing I did to her. She sent me a letter."

"You wrote to her! You wrote to her, and she never told me!" Dr. Katharde put his hands to his head. "I cannot believe it."

"I asked her not to tell, I wasn't ready. But she wanted a reunion between us, you and me, more than anything. She asked me to come up to McIlwain on Wednesday night. I was supposed to wait down in the lecture room for her, and she'd bring you and Edward to me after your meeting upstairs."

"So that's why you were there," whispered Virginia.

"It wasn't a meeting," said Dr. Katharde. "It was a party. She wouldn't have invited you to a party. And if you were so afraid to make yourself known, why would you agree to appear in a public Christmas performance? I was in that pageant. I don't remember seeing you there, Raymond."

Amalya held out his hands pleadingly. "I agreed to take a sick friend's place in the chorus that night. Milton, I was terrified that you'd see me. I saw Edward look at me from the stage—I was sure he knew me, and I started to shake so hard I thought I'd faint. After the pageant, I went straight to the lecture room, and I sat down in the dark, and I closed my eyes to pray—"

"Please, Raymond. I won't be made a fool of."

"I did pray! Then I heard someone, a young woman, shouting for Florence. I thought something was wrong, so I ran into the hall to help her."

"And you attacked her. You knocked her to the floor!"

"I didn't attack her. She ran into me, and I grabbed her to keep from falling. Then we both fell, and she ran away before I could explain."

Virginia shook her head. She took Stephen's arm. "No," she said. "It wasn't like that." She was thinking again of the door, the man charging for her, the blood. She remembered Amalya's voice that night, deep and frightening.

Dr. Katharde moistened his lips. "If you were innocent that night, Raymond, then you would have come upstairs and made yourself known."

"Oh, you think so?" Amalya smiled. "You don't believe me now. Would you have believed me then? I wanted to find Florence, not chat with Howard Molliby." (Dr. Molliby sniffed at this.) "I heard someone coming down the steps. The police would be there soon, I knew that. So I decided to hide until the commotion was over. I ran to the east stairs, climbed up to the fifth floor, and came back down the hall to the attic. And to find it unlocked, well, that seemed like a miracle."

Dr. Katharde sighed. "But you didn't stay there. They tell me you rappelled down to the fire escape on the west side and ran away. Why did you leave if you were innocent?"

Amalya shook his head. "Because I thought I heard someone coming. I had a rope—a belt, actually—from my costume in the play. I tied it around this—what do you call it—parapet?—on the roof and dropped down one floor to the fire escape. Then I walked back to the chapel and met my sons. I'd been planning to do some custodial work after the pageant, but instead we went straight home, that is, to the Viksmas, where we were staying. And I never told them what had happened. I didn't tell anybody till now."

"But, Raymond, you see, I went up and down the west stairs." Dr. Katharde's voice was calm, patient, but unconvinced. "I looked out the stairwell windows. I watched the north and south sides of campus intently. And yet I never saw you during that time."

"You must have been praying, Milton. You must have had your eyes closed for a moment."

"Raymond, I want to believe you. I want to believe you and forgive you."

"Don't believe him!" barked Dr. Molliby at the screen. *"Noli fidem mendaci habere!"*

"Like he said," said Stephen.

"I've been looking for Florence," said Amalya. "I went back yesterday morning in my custodial uniform and searched McIlwain Hall myself, after we swept up for the police. There are hiding places that no one knows about. I wondered if—if someone had killed her and left her there. I couldn't stand to think about it."

"But why did you break the display case that night, and why have you stolen the mask now?"

Amalya hesitated. "The mask?"

"The mask you made and sent to Florence. It was missing this afternoon. We found it at your son's apartment. Can you tell me you didn't put it there?"

"I don't understand. I was in Michigan today. You can ask Myron Erlichson. Remember our old pupil Myron? He's recovering from a fall and can't come, but he advised me to stay in Michigan until Florence was found. Do you know why I didn't take his advice? Do you know why I came back?"

"No." Dr. Katharde stood up and moved a step back from the bed. He looked uncertain, as though he didn't know where to stand.

"Because I heard about Edward," said Amalya. "I wanted to clear Edward. I wanted to talk to you and tell you the truth. I hoped you would believe me. When I got back to Emmet, I found out that one of my younger sons is ill. He needs me here. Florence needs me too."

Dr. Katharde stood staring, shifting slowly from one foot to another.

"Milton, please try to convince them that I haven't done anything. I need to be with my son. And I can help you search for Florence."

"Raymond," Dr. Katharde said quietly, "truthfully, in some ways, I probably rejoiced in your failure. Because I was jealous of your success. It came to you so easily. I acknowledge my own sin, and yet—I cannot believe you, I cannot accept your innocence. I'm not convinced."

"*Gloria deo!*" said Dr. Molliby.

Amalya put his hand over his eyes. "Well, then, I . . . I guess I'm too tired to keep trying."

Dr. Katharde reached over and took Amalya's hand in his own. "Give Florence back to her children."

"Oh, go away now."

Dr. Katharde started slowly away from the bed, his head down. Before he left, he looked around and said quietly, "I will die for her, Raymond, if I have to. I have no family, no one counting on me. Tomorrow is Christmas Eve, and if you will lead us to her, I promise that I will go to my grave before Christmas arrives. If my death is really what you require in order to resurrect her, then my death you shall have." He walked off-screen. Amalya lay still, with his hand over his eyes, breathing heavily. He was a pathetic sight, Virginia thought.

Goodman sighed and turned off the television. "It's late," he said. "I'll talk to Katharde. You folks go home and get some sleep."

"It won't come easily," said Dr. Molliby, "not till that wretch tells us where Florence is."

Virginia stood up from her chair feeling weak. Out in the hall, Dr. Katharde stood slumped over against the cinder-block wall next to the infirmary. Dr. Molliby hurried over to him, and Goodman took him by the arm. "Are you all right, sir?"

He nodded silently.

"You come with me. I'll take you home."

"Virginia," said Stephen as they left the building, "why are you shaking like that?"

"Because it feels like someone's walking on my grave," she said.

13

Walking on Graves

DEEP IN THE NIGHT THE PHONE RANG. It rang and rang, loud enough to wake the dead, but not loud enough to wake Virginia. Wrapped up in blankets, she dreamed that someone was kissing her: Stephen, maybe, or maybe not. "Mmmm. Your moustache tickles." *Moustache?* She heard the phone ringing at last and looked up into a pair of shimmering cat eyes, green lanterns in the dark.

"Miranda."

The cat jumped lightly from the pillow to a chair to the floor. Virginia climbed out of bed not so lightly and followed her out to the kitchen, where Miranda draped across the ringing telephone and flicked her tail. Virginia pushed her away gently. "Hello?"

It was Stephen. "Has Deacon talked to you?"

"No."

"He called me just now and asked me to go over to McIlwain to help."

"Has something happened?"

"I don't know. He said to come over there right away. I'll pick you up in ten minutes."

"Ten minutes? Stephen, I don't even know what time it is." She hung up and slipped down from her chair, sat cross-legged on the floor, and looked at the clock. 3:30 A.M., December 24. Christmas Eve morning.

Even after she bundled up and seated herself on a cold curb outside, she felt as floppy and weak as a beanbag doll. She shut her eyes against the wind and buried her face in her warm gloves, waiting for the rumble of Stephen's mother's Plymouth around the corner.

"Hello?" called a sharp voice. "Hello there, Virginia? Is that you?" Mrs. Viksma stood in a bathrobe and ski parka on the porch behind her. "Do you realize, dear, that it's not even 4:00 in the morning?" She hurried down the steps and across the walk, waving her arms out for balance on a rope of ice. "I heard you marching around upstairs and I thought, *What is that child up to?* I sent you to Chicago yesterday, and since then I haven't had a chance to see you, much less thank you." She paused, as if hoping Virginia might say, "You're welcome," which she didn't, and then said, "You've been coming and going, keeping all kinds of strange hours, barely speaking a word to anyone."

Virginia tried to stir up a reply. "How's the little boy?"

Mrs. Viksma put her hands on her hips. "A little better, thanks to Harold and me."

"Is Arthur with him now?"

"Arthur!" Mrs. Viksma threw up her hands. "I don't know what's become of Arthur. Somebody called him this evening, and then he went away in a panic, said he was going out for a while, hasn't come back."

"Where is their father?" Virginia squinted hard in the dark. She wanted to see whether Mrs. Viksma knew the truth, yet, about Albert Amalya.

"Albert's still in Michigan. Or gone to Timbuktu, for all I know. Borrowed our car to go there and was supposed to bring it back last evening, and I've heard nothing from him. Something is wrong." Mrs. Viksma rolled the word *wrong* around her tongue like a sourball, making a face. "That's why I haven't slept. Something is *wrong,* but young Arthur won't tell me what."

Virginia stared down the street at an icy hump in the black pavement. "Mrs. Viksma, do you know Albert Amalya very well?"

"Why do you ask?"

"I like Arthur. I wondered what you thought of his father."

The landlady hesitated slightly, then said quietly, "Well, he's a charmer all right, that's what I think of him. I took him in as a favor to old friends; now I'm wondering if *they* know him as well as they think they do. I suspect he has a woman somewhere. I'd like to get my car back, if you please; then I'll have better to say about him. But I didn't come out here in the cold to complain." She tightened her shoulders. "I came to check on you. What in the world are you doing on the side of the road at 4:00 in the morning?"

"Waiting for that car," said Virginia, pointing at the Plymouth now on its way down the street, sidling up to the curb. "Goodbye, Mrs. Viksma." She climbed in and pulled the long car door closed behind her. Mrs. Viksma frowned. She waved to them as they pulled away, leaning out toward the street on her tiptoes, staring.

"Good morning," said Stephen in a thick voice. His hair looked as though it had melted overnight and hardened on one side of his head. "I wonder," he said soberly, "whether the police might have found something, whether that's why they've called us over there."

"You think they might have found Florence?" He nodded.

She unrolled her window slightly and took a deep breath. As they swept up toward McIlwain, they saw reporters hovering around the driveway lights. Something was up. Flashlights swung down and over them. Voices flared in the shadows.

They parked low on the front lawn and climbed the hill, passing a small crowd of neighbors watching in pajamas and long coats. As they circled to the back of the building, Virginia looked up to see one window shining bright on the second floor. From the window, Goodman looked down over the crowd. She waved, but he turned without waving back.

"Hey, you two!" Deacon stood in the driveway near the east door, his feet wide apart and his toes pointing in two directions. "I want you upstairs. Come on."

They followed Deacon into the building, up the east steps, and across the fifth floor to the theology department. Virginia had a vision as they entered it: Florence walking into this office, Florence stirring coffee, Florence typing, Florence reading a letter from an atheist—"It's from R.F. He's having doubts—"

"Want coffee?" asked the detective.

"No," said Stephen. "Why don't you tell us what's going on."

"Have you found her?" said Virginia.

Deacon had a withered look in the dim light. "No," he said. "I'm afraid—well, Amalya's escaped."

"Escaped?" said Stephen with a slight laugh, as if it were a joke.

"The doctor who worked on his arm this afternoon gave him some sleeping pills. Amalya must have ground them down and put them in the guard's coffee. Once the idiot was asleep, all he had to do was run out a fire door and disappear. And now we're in deep—what can I say here at Emmet College—deep 'doo-doo.'"

Stephen dropped his head. "Deep doo-doo indeed."

"So what do you do now?" asked Virginia. "If you don't know where he is, he can't lead you to Florence."

"We'll catch up with Amalya," said Deacon. "We've got plenty of help if we need it—state police, more Feds. But it's Christmas Eve, which apparently is a big night for this guy. We're talking about a really twisted person here, walking free. I want to find him immediately."

"He may go back to his family," said Virginia. "Did you try my landlord's house, where his children are staying?"

"He's not there. We've been watching it since we arrested him. The apartment in Chicago is empty. His kid Arthur has been in Emmet since yesterday, and there's no mask, Miss Falls. No mask up there."

"I saw it there."

"It's not there now."

"But I saw it."

"Hey, Deacon," said Goodman, suddenly walking into the office. He nodded at Virginia and Stephen. "Detective, would you mind coming downstairs for a minute?"

"What is it, man?" said Deacon.

Goodman shook his head and turned back to the door. "I'd rather discuss it on the third floor."

Deacon stood up with Stephen and Virginia.

They climbed down two flights and turned right, following Goodman to the broken display case past the other missionary artifacts—a wall arrangement of kimonos and the shaving kits of four alumni martyred in China. Goodman stopped in front of the empty, glassless mask case and held up a clear plastic bag. The hammer hung at an angle inside it. "I've been wondering," he said slowly, "why the kidnapper was carrying this hammer in the first place."

"To break the case and steal the mask," said Deacon. "We know he wanted it because he came back for it later. Probably Mrs. Treadwell caught him in the act."

"That may be," said Goodman. "But why a hammer? Lab tests show material on the handle that matches the dirt right around this building, lots of calcium carbonate leached from the limestone. What was the kidnapper doing before he broke the glass?"

Deacon sniffed and scratched the back of his head.

"Detective," said Goodman, "have we taken a good look in the basement?"

"For Amalya?"

"No, for Mrs. Treadwell."

"Sure we've looked in the basement. I'm not an idiot, Agent."

"I'm starting to think we should look *under* the basement." Goodman turned to Stephen. "Katharde mentioned some rumors about old slave tunnels under this building. Any truth to those?"

"Slave tunnels," said Stephen breathlessly. "Well, the experts say they don't exist, but who knows?"

"Is it true that your first president was an abolitionist?" Goodman said the last word slowly, giving it an extra syllable. Deacon drummed his fingers on his knees.

"He was an abolitionist," said Stephen, "among other things."

"He helped slaves escape before the Civil War? He hid them in tunnels?"

"I have no idea."

"Come on, Agent," said Deacon. "We're not going mining tonight. We'll rule out the basement, and then we turn our attention to Grand Rapids. We know Amalya went there, and we know Erlichson's family was helping him. Maybe he went back to them."

"I think we ought to try a serious dig," said Goodman patiently. "We can start by digging straight under the basement, let's say right under the Tower—that's the oldest section, according to Katharde. What I'd like is an old floor plan of McIlwain, the oldest one available. Can either of you get that for me?" He looked at Virginia and Stephen.

"Are you looking for an entrance to tunnels from the inside?" asked Stephen.

Goodman nodded. "All along, we've been trying to figure out when and how Amalya got Mrs. Treadwell out of the building without being seen. We know he had an alibi for the hour before the party started, so it had to have happened around 8:30, either shortly before or shortly after the time Miss Falls ran into him. Now, we think he left McIlwain through the attic, and, as you know, it seems impossible that a man, even a very strong man, could put a grown woman over his shoulder, lower himself by a rope to a fire escape, and then leave without being seen. Amalya's a big man, but he's an old man, too. My theory is, maybe Mrs. Treadwell never left the building at all. Maybe old Amalya's kept her hidden all this time, till he could use the situation to his best advantage."

"To get revenge on his old friends," mumbled Virginia, "or maybe to get revenge on God, if there is a God."

Deacon snorted. "Why don't we spend our time on a few other leads first? We need to talk to Amalya's kid, obviously, because I'm betting he knows how the mask got out of his apartment and where it is now."

"So bring him in," said Goodman. "I'll head up the dig personally. I've got a few people coming in to help."

"Feds," said Deacon, putting his hand to his stomach.

"I can get my mother to open up the library archives." said Stephen. "She'd know where to look for a map."

"We can use you around here," said Goodman. "I'd like a look in those archives, myself.

I'll get your mother. Miss Falls, you want to show me the way?"

She felt Stephen's eyes on her. "I'll go with you," she said. Minutes later, she and Goodman were back in the cold, working their way among the cameras to his car.

"So you don't think there's a God?" Goodman said as he let her in.

The question took her by surprise. "Why, do you?"

"Yes, I think there's probably a God."

She smiled nervously. "I guess I don't. He might be out there, but I've never had a sense of Him, not the way some people do."

"That's honest enough," said Goodman. "Don't say you're Abe Lincoln's friend if you never even shook his hand."

"Right."

They drove down the hill, over the tracks, to the Holcs' driveway. "You wait here," he said. In a minute, he returned with Stephen's mother. She had a toothbrush in her mouth. She wore flannel pajamas, a heavy coat, and tennis shoes. "Mrs. Holc," said Goodman casually as she climbed in, "do you think that there are tunnels under McIlwain Hall?"

"Absolutely," she said without hesitation, so quickly that he laughed. "What's so funny?" she said. "All you need to do is read the memoirs of Rafis Johansen."

"Who?"

"Rafis Johansen Fawcett. The one they named

that chapel for. Her mother was a runaway slave back before the Civil War. The family resettled in Liberia, but Dr. Johansen came back here to study. She went overseas as a missionary and then returned and actually taught Bible and Greek at Emmet—the college's only black professor before the First World War. Shocked the town to pieces, don't you know. Married a white businessman, Frederick James Fawcett. They traveled around and gave lectures."

"What did she have to do with the tunnels?" asked Goodman.

"Dr. Johansen claimed she had been inside them as a little girl. It's all in her memoirs, up there in the archives. Of course, you have to know where to look."

"Do you know where to look?"

"Certainly." She took a pair of gloves from her purse. She pulled them on, then put on sunglasses, which reflected the oncoming headlights perfectly. "I don't want a headache," she said. "I haven't even had breakfast yet."

Goodman glanced at Virginia. She tapped the side of her head.

They pulled up behind the library. Mrs. Holc walked slightly ahead of them. She let them in at the loading entrance, then took them up to Special Collections on a staff elevator. When the doors opened, she pointed at a distant wall. There in the dark was the coffin. Above it hung the picture Virginia had noticed before, the portrait of an old man.

"Who is that?" asked Goodman.

"Herbert McIlwain," said Mrs. Holc. "The Johansen memoirs are in the coffin, along with other materials on the college founders."

"Was the coffin ever used?" asked Virginia, horrified.

"It sat in McIlwain's office. He was a strange and morbid man, lived in that little shack near the Tower and built coffins, when he wasn't preaching or hunting. He made this for himself, but when he died, his family took him downstate for burial in a very fancy mausoleum and this one came to the college. Now it holds his papers. Grim, isn't it?"

Goodman thrust his hands in his pockets and coughed. "Can we get a light? How about it?"

"Certainly." Mrs. Holc stepped away to find a light, and Virginia exchanged a quick look with Goodman.

"Future mother-in-law?" he whispered.

She smiled, embarrassed, but didn't answer.

"All right," said Mrs. Holc, coming back. "This box is never locked." She put her fingers under the lid and pried it open. Inside were piles of decaying brown papers, some thrown here and there, some wrapped up carefully in plastic bags. Mrs. Holc dug her hands down inside, and a smell arose, a smell of earth and sweat. She brought out a stack of old diaries, water-stained and bent.

"Here they are. You'll find drawings in there, somewhere. I've seen them." She handed the books to Goodman. He handed them to Virginia.

"I want to get back to that dig," he said. "Call me if you find something."

"All right." She felt a little disappointed. She watched him disappear into the shelves, then sat down at a table in the reading room and spread the books out in front of her. "I wonder if I should try to find a map, instead of looking at these. That's what I came for."

"I'll look for the map, sweetie," said Mrs. Holc, walking back into the shelves. "You read." Virginia listened to her footsteps, the soft squeak of tennis shoes and the swish of a coat against the shelves. She took a startled breath and put her hands to her ears, remembering Wednesday night: Lucy Trapp's sharp footsteps outside the department, Dr. Katharde's hysteria over finding the room decorated for a party, Dr. Nimitz's shock on finding guests crouching in a dark office, Dr. Erlichson's voice outside the window. Most of all, she remembered Raymond Treadwell in the dark.

> I cannot say exactly how we achieved our arrival at the underground hotel . . .

Virginia's eyes stopped on the word *underground*. She pulled the book closer.

> . . . only that we came curled up like animals in boxes, sucking cold air through tiny holes. We ascended to the clouds and then climbed down to hell by means of a narrow,

winding staircase, as one might do in a
nightmare. Being a child, I imagined that
demons had buried me there, deep under
the graves of white men. For three days and
three nights I lay in the belly of the earth,
staring at a flickering candle. My mother
sat across from me, staring at the same candle, nursing my baby sister. Periodically,
our white friend and his wife came and
went with provisions. Then at last we
walked straight out to a small place in the
open air and had a quick look at the stars;
a bell rang as we rode away that night in
a covered carriage.

She read it again. Here was the description of
a tunnel, deep underground, that must be
reached by a long climb and then a long descent
down a winding staircase. Could that staircase
still be there?

"Mrs. Holc?" she called out.

"Ye-e-e-s?"

"Has McIlwain been remodeled since 1859?"

"Oh yes. We've kept up with modern times.
In some respects, anyway. Of course, we do
store our archival papers in coffins. There's
something rather medieval about that."

"Mrs. Holc, did you find an old floor plan?"

"Oh, darling, I have found an entire book of
floor and grounds plans, and I'll bring it to you.
However, it won't help. There are no tunnels
shown here."

Virginia took the book of plans in one arm and the Johansen memoirs in the other. "I'm taking these back to McIlwain."

Mrs. Holc pulled her sunglasses down from the top of her head. "And I'm going home to bed," she said. "Call me when you do find a tunnel. But not before eight."

"Thank you." Virginia hurried out the reading-room door, through the archives, and down the back stairs. She left the library and crossed campus quickly, passing between Fawcett Chapel and the conservatory to get to McIlwain. Though the pavement was slick, she began to run, gripping the books, trying not to fall.

14

Descent

NIGHT HAD EDGED UP LIKE A WINDOW
shade over the ball fields east of McIlwain. Virginia saw the first white line of dawn from the
windows on the fifth floor. She had expected to
find the police still here, still hashing out details
of the search, but instead she came upon a dark
Department of Theology, abandoned in a hurry.
Chairs sat pushed aside or pushed over, fast-
food wrappers lay balled up around the trash
can—missed shots. She assumed that Goodman
and Deacon had headed to the basement, and
she started out the door into the hall again.

As she turned to the door, she heard bits of
conversation from Dr. Nimitz's office: Dr.
Katharde talking with Dr. Molliby. Their voices
rose. She paused to listen.

"I can't stand it!" cried Dr. Katharde. "I can't

stand to hear you put me above him! I was as guilty as he for letting the evil go on so long! I knew that he had removed himself from God. I chalked it up to his misery. I overlooked it for the sake of friendship and, even worse, convenience. And then he assaulted Lucy—"

"That was years ago," said Dr. Nimitz. Virginia strained to hear his thin, sad voice. "You've asked forgiveness, haven't you, Milton?"

"My repentance accomplishes nothing, Edward, with Florence in the grave. I honestly feel that I owe more than that. I owe my life! And you, Howard, I know you've been jealous of him all these years, *shamed* by the way he treated you. You've never let go of your own pride. According to Christ, you've committed murder many times, hating Raymond in your heart."

"Preposterous," said Dr. Molliby. "What do you plan to do, Milton, jump out of a window in hopes of bringing her back? Your actions will only be absorbed into the structure of what is— there's no sense doing anything foolish. She may be with God already. We have to find another way to deal with Raymond. He's toying with us. He only wants to make us suffer more."

"Poor Raymond," said Dr. Nimitz. "He's an outcast now. When I think of the pain he must feel—looking for joy in bitterness."

"There's no joy in anything," said Dr. Katharde. Virginia heard the tears in his voice. "No joy in anything."

A long silence followed.

"Virginia?" A soft voice from the hall startled her. Stephen stood nearby. "What are you doing? The police are downstairs."

"I'm not doing anything." She stepped out and shut the office door, shaking.

"Are you all right?"

"Yes. Here, take one of these books, would you?"

"Certainly. You don't look good. Lean on me."

They walked down the hall together, to the west stairs. Virginia felt her legs give way. Stephen caught her, held her on her feet, then set her down gently at the top of the steps.

"You need to eat something, you idiot." He patted her on the head like a cat. "There are doughnuts downstairs. Deacon brought them. I told him he fit the stereotype."

"I'm not hungry. I need to talk to Lucy if she's still in town. I need to ask her about something."

"Sure, we'll find her," he said quickly, before she could go on. "Now be quiet and just sit there for a minute, get your breath. I'll be right back."

"Stephen!" she said, sitting up to talk to him as he started down the steps. "Where are the others? Where's Goodman? Where's Deacon?"

"Goodman's in the basement, digging. Deacon's out looking for Arthur Amalya. Didn't you notice my clothes?" He pointed at his black knees and shoes and smiled.

"Stephen—," she began, without really looking at him. She wanted to tell him about the conversation she'd just heard in the department.

"Yes?" he said. "What?"

"Um—" She remembered the maps and held out the folders. "Your mother helped me find these. They're for Goodman."

"What are they?"

"Diaries of a woman who says she was once in the tunnels under this building. Can you take the book downstairs right away? He'll want it."

"Yeah, but I'm worried about you. You promise to sit there till I get back?"

She lifted her head and looked straight above at the pale skylight over the stairs. "Oh, I guess so."

"I'm bringing you a doughnut." Stephen headed down, two steps at a time. She watched him round a corner, then heard his footsteps dropping away, away, becoming distant and then silent.

A wind rattled the door nearest her. A cold breeze rushed around her wrists and ankles. Someone must have left a window up somewhere. She got up slowly, found a classroom open, and went in to check. No windows open here, but looking out she saw a projection of the roof and recognized it as the place where Amalya had lowered himself by a rope to the fire escape, while Dr. Katharde was watching another window. She looked at it for a long time, then went back to the hall.

She kept going—past the department, past the central stairs, through the seminar room, to the other side of the building. Though she did feel weak, hungry too, a suspicion drove her on. She kept repeating those words in her mind: *"We ascended to the clouds and then climbed down to hell by means of a narrow, winding staircase, as one might do in a nightmare. Being a child, I imagined that demons had buried me there, deep under the graves of white men."*

The attic door stood wide open. She went inside and pulled on the string light. She hadn't noticed all the big wire cages before, full of bits and pieces—a wardrobe without doors, a couch without cushions, a bicycle without wheels. Mostly junk up here.

Behind the cages, on the plywood walls, she read some of the graffiti: "Robert and Rebeccah dedicate their marriage to the Lord, April, 1949." "My Karen—Fairer than flowers, lovely in spring, dearer than almost anything." What exactly was she looking for? A secret panel. A trap door. Maybe under one of these big cages. She tried to push one out of place; it shrieked an inch across the floor and stopped, blocked by a beam. "Oh, forget it," she said aloud. "Anyway, there's nothing under this floor but the sociology department." She needed to go further up into the attic, into the Tower itself.

She climbed the steps and walked over a bridge to the second level. It was too dark up here to see much; the light from the lower attic was faint and yellow. Her knees were shaking. She dropped to the dusty planks of the bridge and sat for a moment in the dark, thinking. Then she heard something—a noise farther up, through a doorway. A flashlight flickered briefly from that direction. She crawled to the nearby flight of steps and looked over the top.

There he is. In the next level of the attic, a flashlight shifted slowly from wall to wall. It rippled across beams and poles, over foam, over boards and crumbling brick until it shone, miles away, on the words *No Resurrection.*

Virginia dug her nails into the old, soft wood of the steps. The flashlight suddenly skipped backwards over the foam and settled on the bridge. Then it danced over a yellow police rope. It bounced over several thin boards that stretched from beam to beam across insulation. The police had climbed over to that far wall to collect evidence. They had left a makeshift bridge behind.

Somewhere far away in the building, Virginia heard a jackhammer. The man on the bridge put the flashlight under his left arm. It lit up his broad face, carving deep shadows around his eyes. *Treadwell,* thought Virginia.

He started forward, and each time he stepped from one board to another, she heard a spring and a crack as the wood strained under his weight. He shone the light on the far wall, keeping it on the words *No Resurrection.*

Virginia noticed again the graffiti trailing un-

derneath. *Beulah, Aaronsen, Fawcett* . . . It
struck her then. Fawcett was the name that
Rafis Johansen had taken when she married a
white man from the town. Did Raymond
Treadwell know?

Treadwell grunted, struggling to pull out
boards. He had a crowbar with him. She
glimpsed it as the flashlight fell from under his
arm and landed on the insulation nearby. The
light lit up the full wall and frightened a bat
swinging under the rafters. The bat squealed and
fluttered to another corner.

Virginia began to crawl forwards again in the
dark, knee to hand, knee to hand, quietly. Treadwell was a good twenty yards away, but what
if he heard her and came running back? How
would she get away from him in the dark?

A board groaned as he ripped it down from
the wall. A second board groaned and fell into
the insulation, across the path of the flashlight.

The light skipped across Treadwell's face for
just a moment, and down his shirt. Then he held
it into the hole he'd made. A gash gleamed suddenly; red brick showed through, like a sore
throat. He lifted one big leg and threw it over,
then dipped down and vanished into the wall.
The room turned cold and black.

"The tunnel," Virginia said softly. "Now what
do I do?" She could run back and find the others—through the attic in the dark and then five
flights down. Florence might be dead by then.
Or she could keep going, make her way across

the police bridge—*Of course,* she thought, *that will probably include my falling through the ceiling of the seminar room below*—and follow Amalya down. She crawled forwards.

She inched along, standing now, but hunched over, feeling with the toes of her shoes for planks overlapping this one. Before her foot touched anything, her hand brushed against a ribbon—the police rope, probably. The other bridge must be here somewhere—there.

She climbed under the side rail and stepped onto it. Plywood bounced underneath her. *Yell for help? Create a stir? No. What if I put Florence in danger?* She kept going until warmer, musty air flew up around her ears. Her fingers touched sharp boards.

She leaned forward and put her head in the hole to listen. No voices, but the air wailed like the sea in a shell. She was high above the fifth floor of McIlwain. The tunnel must be far, far down. *Below the graves of white men.*

But Rafis Johansen had also spoken of a winding staircase. Virginia gritted her teeth and put her leg through the wall.

Her foot met nothing.

She gripped the wood and lowered herself farther, farther, waiting to meet something solid, casting around wildly for a rung or a stairstep.

She went further down until she hung in the air by just one knee bent over the opening, her fingers dug in tight. Still, she met nothing solid. She would have to bring her leg over and hang by her hands alone. A chill spread across her scalp and down her neck. She'd never be able to pull herself back up. She couldn't do it.

And then came a scream, rising up like a dark bird from far down. It rang like a bell in Virginia's ears, and the next thing she knew, her leg was over and she was falling. Her fingers raked ladder rungs as she fell, but she couldn't get hold. Her back hit a wall, and she went head over heels around a coil of steps, into something hard. Below, she heard the scream again: more muffled now, and distant.

She lay still for a moment, feeling dizzy, feeling a sharp pain in her side. She wanted to scream, not knowing where she was or what she'd done to herself. When she pulled up, the pain sharpened like a spear between her ribs. Something warm streamed into her eyes. She opened her mouth and tasted blood.

The staircase twirled around tightly. Virginia went down as quickly as she could, easing from step to step, her hand on her burning side, her back against the brick wall. The jackhammer began again and grew louder and louder until it sounded just a wall away, as if she could have knocked on the bricks and shouted for Goodman or Stephen. But she kept going down, and the hammer grew far away again. She must be fifteen feet below basement level now, maybe more. *Search in light, you search in vain.* With her eyes open wide, she landed on dirt and shuffled forwards carefully, expecting another step.

Which way had Treadwell gone? Where was Florence? *She's buried under McIlwain.* She turned back and forth, unsure now even of where the steps were. She stepped forwards and walked into them. *Go the other way.*

The only sound was her own breathing, her footsteps. But as she moved forwards, she began to see a slight glow to her right. Was someone there? She inched on quickly, stretching her hands out.

Thirty slow paces and the glow was only a little bit brighter. She felt a slight puff of air against her cheek. Ten more feet, and then, as if the wall had rolled back suddenly like a black curtain, she saw a lantern sitting on the ground. Near it were several knotted ropes, not untied but sliced apart—so he had a knife with him. A loaf of bread and a Coke bottle sat near the lantern, too, and a bucket that she knew better than to look inside; an acrid odor filled the room. She picked up the lantern and stared around briefly.

The room was a man-made cave, a section of an old mine shaft braced by huge beams of wood that looked ready to buckle. There was little air, but stepping into the wider tunnel she felt again a slight, cool breath against her cheek. The air was sweeter, and there was more of it. The lantern flame perked up, and the tunnel, as she followed it farther, rose gently toward the surface.

There had to be an exit from the other end, too.

Maybe Treadwell had already taken Florence to the surface. What did he intend to do with her?

Virginia started to run. The incline grew sharper. The tunnel narrowed until it was just a crawlspace. She got on her hands and knees and crawled forwards. Her ribs throbbed.

Suddenly, just ahead, she saw a dim pattern of lights on the floor of the crawlspace. The lights formed a rough circle, about the circumference of a softball. Probably a drain. She crept toward it, turned on her back, and looked up into an empty, tiled room. A small, high skylight stood propped open, far away. It was apparently the end of the line. The passage ahead was too narrow even for crawling. Where was Treadwell? *Probably wedged somewhere in this stupid tunnel,* she thought.

She backed up. Then she remembered the boards that had blocked the tunnel entrance up in the Tower. Treadwell had known just where to pry them away. Maybe the same thing applied here. She didn't have a crowbar, but she could check for a loose board, feel for a loose nail.

She began to inch around, pushing up with her knees and hands. Time was getting short. She stopped pushing and started to kick and punch, bringing dirt down in her face.

About three feet back from the drain, her foot rammed straight up into the open air, and a pair of thick boards flew over and crashed on the tile. She shimmied down that way and stuck the lantern up through the hole, then her head and shoulders. "What?" she said, and her voice echoed on tile. "A bathroom?" She sat for a moment, looking from an open closet door over the surface of a public rest room—a *men's* rest room, judging by the plumbing. She hoisted her whole self out and found the door, then raced outside into an empty hall. It was the chapel. She'd come out in Fawcett Chapel.

The nearest exit was through a classroom, around a corner, up two steps. She ran, holding her sides, wincing every time she took a breath. She pulled the heavy door open and looked out. There, on the conservatory lawn, between McIlwain and the chapel, in front of a cloud of reporters and onlookers, stood Raymond Treadwell.

In front of him, blindfolded and haggard, stood Florence. Her hair was matted with dried blood. He held her by one wrist, a knife in his right hand. Dr. Katharde watched from a fifth-floor window.

"Look, Milton," yelled Treadwell. "She's alive!"

"Get the police!" Virginia shouted. "Somebody get Goodman!"

"Everybody calm down! Calm down!" shouted Treadwell, glancing angrily back her way. "Just keep away from me!"

Cameras flashed but the reporters moved back, and then, from a fifth-floor window, came a shout. Treadwell looked up. Florence looked up. Virginia looked up.

"Take me!" Dr. Katharde shouted. "Don't take her life! Take mine!"

"No, I'm not going to hurt her," said Treadwell. "I rescued her! I cut her loose!" He reached toward her, but Virginia was already running for him.

She leaped onto his back, locked her arms around his big neck, and squeezed as hard as she could. He pitched back and forth, choking, but she held on.

"No!" someone shouted from the door of the east wing. Virginia glanced up and saw Goodman running toward them with Stephen just behind.

A shot boomed above.

Virginia looked up as Dr. Katharde melted across the window frame, his arms dangling down like locks of hair.

Raymond Treadwell screamed and fell forwards. Virginia tumbled onto her side.

"Dr. Katharde!" she said. "Help Dr. Katharde!" Stephen knelt beside her. Goodman pushed Treadwell down and handcuffed him, while a few feet away, Florence lay weeping on the ground.

15

An Interview with the Victim

"VIRGINIA?" SAID STEPHEN.

She opened her eyes and saw him standing over her, his eyebrows darting around anxiously, his golden hair tilted forwards on his frowning forehead. The high white walls to either side of him reminded her of the sanctuary of the First United Methodist Church of North Tallahassee. For a second she thought she was at a funeral.

"Is Dr. Katharde dead?" she said weakly.

"No." He shook his head.

"Is he hurt?"

"No, he's not hurt." Stephen let a second pass and then said, "Virginia, it was an act."

"What?"

He moved away from the bed to sit down on

a chair. "Katharde had this idea that he'd die in Florence's place."

"I know."

"Well, he had a pistol with him—he was actually going to shoot himself. But he changed his mind at the last minute. He held the pistol between his arm and his chest and fired at the floor."

"I'm glad he's not hurt." She put her hand to her side. It was bandaged tightly, still tender.

"He got a burn, that's all. You're the only one we're worried about."

"Where am I, exactly?"

"You're at Emmet City Hospital. You have a couple of broken ribs and some stitches in your hard little skull, and I'm here fulfilling my Christian duty to the sick."

"My side is killing me. My head, too."

"I'm not surprised. Deacon told me you must have dropped eight feet through that hole in the attic. Treadwell's so big, he broke the old ladder down from the wall before you climbed in. You went out cold right after you *wrestled*—" he hung on this word—"him to the ground. Then they doped you up for stitches and whatnot. But you're O.K. The doctor says you just need a lot of sleep. And some nutrition, for Pete's sake."

"I don't want to stay here."

"You get to go home tomorrow."

"I don't want to go home, either." She was thinking of Florida. She put her hand to her head and felt a hard, sore seam, a zipper in her skull. "I want to go back to the Viksmas," she said, "or somewhere else, but not home. Does my family know about this?"

"I called them a few hours ago. They should be on the plane by now."

"What?"

"I'm kidding. I haven't told anyone. Of course, it's possible your family will see you on television *wrestling—*" he hung on the word again—"a 230-pound man to the ground."

"I didn't wrestle anyone. He fell when he heard that shot. How about Florence? How's she?"

"She's with her family, I guess. It'll be Christmas in two hours." He looked at his watch. "Nice Christmas present for them."

"And what about Amalya?"

"Goodman shot him in the knee. I don't know where he is now. Somewhere very uncomfortable, I hope."

"Back in the tunnel," she said slowly, narrowing her eyelids. "That's where I would put Raymond Treadwell. Back down in the cold, in the dark, in the grave. That's where he belongs. Break down those ladders and seal up those holes."

"Let him play poker with the other rats," Stephen said. He sat forwards on his chair.

Virginia couldn't smile. "No forgiveness, no atonement, and no resurrection. Stephen, I feel terrible."

Stephen poured her a glass of water. He

propped her pillow up, moved close, and held her head against his side as she drank. In the lamplight, the shadow of the water's rim made waves across his wrist. "You can come to my house," he said. "My mother and I will take good care of you."

On the lamp table by the bed, a flesh-colored phone rang. They both looked at it. It had lipstick stains on the receiver. Maybe other patients blew kisses on it to those they loved. Stephen picked it up. "Hello. Oh, hello there!" He put his hand over the mouthpiece. "It's Florence, Ginny."

She felt sicker, suddenly, filled with dread. "Tell her I'm sleeping. I'll call her later."

"Aw, come on, talk to her."

"I can't right now." Virginia pushed her head down against her flat pillow.

He frowned and waited. "Why not?"

"I'm in the hospital. Do I need another excuse?"

He sighed and put the receiver to his ear again. "Can she call you back, Mrs. Treadwell? No, don't worry, she'll call you tomorrow." He hung up the phone and stared at her. "I've learned a lot about you in the last few days," he said.

"Oh yeah, like what?"

"You're braver and kinder than you first appear."

"Thank you."

"But you're also kind of uptight, Virginia.

You're sometimes dishonest, and always stubborn. I didn't know that before."

"Love is blind," she said.

"I can't believe you'd refuse to see the woman whose life you just saved. All she wants to do is thank you."

"I'm not up to it. She'll expect me to be emotional."

"And you can't be, can't you?"

"Stephen, I'm sick. Give me a break, I'm not at my best."

"But if you always avoid emotions, if you don't let yourself give in to pain or happiness or gratitude or whatever—"

"What horrible things will happen to me, Stephen?"

"You'll be alone all your life."

"Oh, I understand what you're saying, believe me. You just want me to give in to you. You think if you can break me down, you'll have me."

"Right," he said, sticking his chin out.

"Well, that's selfish."

"Maybe so. I don't apologize for such selfishness. I'd like you to be equally selfish about me. That kind of selfishness makes the world go around."

She rubbed her eyes. "I don't want to be possessed. I don't want to possess anyone. I want to do my own thing. You can follow me around with your tail wagging if you want to, but I'm a cat person, Stephen. I don't like to be owned."

He sighed. "Even a cat needs a warm place to sleep." He leaned down to kiss her gently on the lips. "Miranda gives me more affection than you do."

"Hey, come get me tomorrow, O.K.? Come get me. Take me to your house for Christmas. And don't forget my present, either. Yours might be the only one I get."

She heard him humming a Mozart piano concerto as he went down the hall. In a few seconds, her eyes closed, and she was almost asleep. But her lips moved gently. "Stephen," she whispered. "Stephen, Albert, Rafis." All those names, and for every name a face, and for every face a name, and a cave like a mouth speaking quietly in the wall of the attic, two words: *No Resurrection.* In the dead of night she woke to see a nurse standing over her with a pair of white pills in a Dixie cup. She slept for another two hours, then woke to see the same nurse waiting to take her temperature. Two hours later, the poor woman had bags under her eyes and another Dixie cup in her hand. "I'm off in ten minutes," she said. "Heard on T.V. you're a lifesaver. God bless and hope you have a good recovery."

"Thank you."

Early in the morning, Virginia couldn't sleep any longer. She lay quietly staring at a mute T.V. high in the corner. Every half-hour or so, McIlwain loomed across the screen, and she glimpsed a quick shot of herself on Albert

Amalya's back, riding him rodeo-style. The reporters had been quick with their cameras—she saw Goodman shooting, Dr. Katharde in the window, Florence on the ground. It all looked so rehearsed now, so safe, so small-budget. Yet when she flicked the television off, her heart started to race.

An elderly man in a white coat came in suddenly without knocking.

"You're the girl, aren't you?" he said.

"I think so. Are you the doctor?"

"I am. You can be discharged anytime you want. The nurse will explain your medication."

"Yes, sir."

He doddered away. A male attendant explained in a Midwestern accent how one took a shower after breaking two ribs: "Grup the seefty bare as so with the luft heyund. . . ." The attendant departed, casting curious glances over his shoulder, and Virginia started to undress. She'd pulled off everything but her slippers when a knock came at the door. She slowly wound her sheets around her again and sat back in the chair by the bed. "Who is it?"

"Virginia?"

She knew the voice immediately but couldn't name it. *My mother?* she thought for a moment. A throb came up in her throat, like a pain trying to climb out of her heart. It was Florence. "Come in."

Florence put her head around the door. "Merry Christmas, dear Virginia." She continued to stand behind the door, leaning forward, waiting.

"Really, come in."

"Thank you," she said and limped in slowly. Her head was bandaged. Bracelets of white cloth circled her wrists, where the ropes had been. She hugged Virginia tight around the neck and kissed her hard on the cheek. "I had to come," she said in a whisper, not letting go. She said it into Virginia's ear, and though it felt nice, like a kiss from a child, Virginia blushed. "I asked Milton to bring me. I had to say thank you. I owe you so much."

"You don't owe me anything."

"You risked your life for me," said Florence. "You and Milton. I wanted to be with you this morning, because you've been with me in spirit all these dark days—" She started to cry. "Also, I just feel that I owe you an explanation." She sat down. "Because I brought this on everyone."

"I already know what I need to know," said Virginia. "I only blame the person who's hurt you."

Florence shook her head. "Raymond was a very good man when I married him. There couldn't have been a better husband, anywhere. That's why I let him fool me this time. I thought he could be himself again if I loved him enough. He really made me believe he loved me again. I'm so sorry, Virginia. It's all my fault."

"I'm sorry for you," said Virginia, shaking her head. She felt as though she might cry herself.

"I started getting letters from Raymond in September, saying he was back in the country and doing well. He even called me on the telephone once. He sounded so nice. I missed him. I thought I would ask him to meet me for the first time along with Milton and Edward and Howard, just to be on the safe side—to get their opinion, too. Milton was always warning me that Raymond might come back and try to charm me. Milton, you know, he worried that I was too trusting."

"Did you tell anyone what you were planning?" asked Virginia.

"I didn't tell anyone but you—that is, I told you about the Christmas party, dear. I wanted it to be a surprise for everyone, but I knew that the greatest surprise, for good or ill, would come afterwards, at least for us old-timers. I wrote Raymond a letter inviting him to meet us and to have a true reconciliation. I told him to wait down in the lecture hall until I brought the others to him—at around 9:30 or 10:00, when the party was finishing. And I knew, I just knew, that he would never dare to face Milton unless he had truly changed in heart and soul. He called and said he'd come. Well, I was so very, very happy. But when I went up Wednesday night to take the food for the party, I happened to see the mask he'd given me hanging on the tree in the department, and I just didn't understand why it was there. I thought it was some sort of prank."

Virginia winced. Florence touched the bandages on her wrists. "I carried it back downstairs," she said, "so that it wouldn't upset Milton, you know, because he's always hated it. Just as I was putting it away, someone came up behind me and hit me over the head. *Now* I know that it was Raymond. I never even heard or saw him. I just felt that blow. And he carried me down to that hole and kept me blindfolded and let me sit there in the dark, cold underground for days, just like an animal. He brought me food and water twice, but—" Florence let out a sob. "It was bad enough the first time, when he tried to hurt us all, but to know that he could be so hateful and deceiving even after all these years—how is it possible?"

"Did you tell anyone he'd written you?" said Virginia.

"Not a soul. I was afraid to. I thought they'd talk me out of seeing him. I had dreams, Virginia, of the two of us ringing the Tower bell again, the way we did years ago when we announced our wedding. He gave me a set of keys to the Tower that day, with our initials on them. I kept them with me. He must have stolen them from me in order to take me down to that horrible, horrible place and leave me there. Oh, Virginia, we've come so far from that beautiful day in the Tower. How could we have come so far?"

"I don't know." Virginia had a different question. She squeezed her hands together, but it made her side ache and she felt herself grimace as she said, "Don't leave quite yet. There's something bothering me."

Florence nodded. "Yes, dear?"

"May I ask you something?"

"All right, but I may not—" Florence put her fists up to her eyes.

"Maybe they didn't tell you, but somehow most of your keys got into my purse on Wednesday night. I threw them down to Dr. Erlichson by accident. This was after you disappeared."

"Mark Erlichson?"

"Yes."

"Well, I don't understand that either," said Florence. "I had them when I went to put the mask away. I'm sure Raymond took them."

"Is there any chance—I know it's ridiculous—but is there *any* chance that someone else was in on this?"

"You mean one of those sons of his?"

"Or one of us?" Virginia held her eyes steady. "Like Mark Erlichson or Dr. Nimitz . . ."

Florence's mouth dropped. "Of course not."

"I'm not saying anything."

"No, no one even knew about Raymond, Virginia. I usually tore up his letters."

"Usually?"

"Just to be cautious. I wrote him my last letter from my own kitchen—no, oh no, I suppose I did write it at the office on Friday during my coffee break, but then I was very careful. I didn't make a copy or a carbon. I mailed it with the other invitations from home."

"But could he—I mean, Raymond—have made contact with one of the professors? Could he have asked someone for help?"

"You don't know what you're saying, dear. It's unthinkable. Few people would help Raymond Treadwell. Because he's hurt or betrayed practically everyone—"

"What about Dr. Erlichson? Your husband told Dr. Katharde he's been spending time with Dr. Erlichson's uncle in Grand Rapids. They're old friends, right?"

Florence nodded. "Good friends."

"Well, the Erlichsons have been helping him out. And it's strange—the night I went to decorate for the party, Dr. Erlichson's office light was on. Maybe he'd just left it on. But maybe he was there, saw the decorations, and figured something out."

"Oh, no. Oh, I don't know. I'm so confused." She started to cry again and bent over the bed. Just as Virginia looked around for the tissue box, a knock came at the door. Florence's daughter Merrel walked in slowly, hugging her purse. "Mother," she said, leaning down to the side of the bed, "Uncle Milton's waiting downstairs."

"Doesn't he want to see Virginia?" Florence said from the sheets.

"He's tired. I think he needs rest."

"No, Merrel, I want to stay with Virginia. Till she's all right."

"Mother, you need rest and so does Miss

Falls. Come along home. Your grandchildren are waiting to see you."

Florence lifted up and limped from the room. Virginia raised the head of her bed and waved.

After they left, Virginia thought hard, gathering up all the events of the last week and laying them out before her. She thought of Lucy Trapp, the keys, the Grand Rapids bank account, and Mark Erlichson's uncle. (And how much did Mark know about it all?) Her thoughts became a knot, and the knot was a knot in a long rope of revelations, something to grip as she climbed down, slowly, toward the truth underneath.

16

Arthur Amalya

THIN BLACK TREES SKIPPED ALONG BE-side the car windows, framing the world in moving pictures. It was Christmas noon, slightly warmer than the day before. The sun cast deep shadows in the snow around Emmet doorways, under awnings and porches, under juniper and holly. Driving past McIlwain, Virginia and Stephen looked up at the deserted campus.

"Reporters left a mess," he said. "Front lawn is gray mush."

"What did you expect them to do? Put the snow back?" She pulled her jacket tight around her shoulders, feeling unusually chilled in spite of the slight thaw. For just a moment she did miss home—mostly the weather, and of course her mother. It was Christmas. Hard not to miss your mother on Christmas Day.

"You're coming to my house for Christmas dinner," Stephen said. "Don't argue."

"I won't."

He dropped her off at the Viksmas' so she could change her clothes and promised to be back in an hour. She climbed carefully up the stairs. She felt weak, and the stairs were slick. As her right foot hit the top step, she heard the Viksmas' door swing open below and footsteps on the porch.

"Virginia Falls?"

"Yes, Mrs. Viksma?"

Mrs. Viksma came to the foot of the steps in a dull green skirt and white sneakers, hugging something around her shoulders that was either a blanket or a tablecloth. She had a harsh, hurt look, as if someone about to take her picture had said, "O.K., Harriet, hon, try to look *betrayed.*"

"Someone wants to speak to you," she said coolly.

Virginia hesitated, thinking of the portraits on the television set. "Your sons? They're home for Christmas, aren't they?"

She shook her head quickly. "My sons have gone driving with their father. Don't expect to see much of them. No, Arthur's waiting. He's been in a terrible depression since yesterday. Can you come down a moment?"

Virginia nodded and caught her breath. Something tightened her ribs like the jerk of a cord. She came carefully back down, counting every step. Mrs. Viksma watched until she reached the bottom, then opened the front door and called out, "Arthur, Virginia Falls is here! Come in, Virginia."

The house was bright and had the sociable smell of pot roast, but Virginia felt an uneasy quiet as she came through the door. Mrs. Viksma pointed her into the living room. She'd been in here many a time before. She knew to step over the ferns on her way to the couch, to duck under the philodendrons. Her boots made no noise on the thick green carpet as she walked in. She sat on an overstuffed green couch and looked through a green-curtained window at the yard outside. Where were the little boys? with Mr. Viksma?

Raymond Treadwell's oldest son entered the room alone, staring straight down. He looked like a preacher in his white shirt and black tie.

"Arthur," she said.

He stood a moment, his hands in his pockets, his lips flickering in and out. "I've been talking to the police. Do you think they'll send my father to prison?"

She wished they could just make small talk for a minute, shoot the breeze while she got her words together. She squeezed her hands together.

"He may have hurt people in the past, he may have done wrong. But my father is innocent."

She tried to meet his eyes. The room was so bright. "But you saw him with her. He had a weapon. He would have hurt her if the police hadn't shot him."

Arthur raised his thin shoulders and let them drop. "He wanted to set her free, not hurt her. Don't you see that he rescued the woman?"

"Arthur, Florence was his wife. He put her underground for four days in order to get revenge on his old friends."

Arthur shook his head. "He doesn't want revenge."

"Then how do you explain what happened?" Her cheeks felt hot.

"Somebody else put her down there! I think it was the person who wanted revenge on my father, the same one who blackmailed Mrs. Treadwell."

"The one who blackmailed her?" She sighed. "Maybe you're talking about the money she gave Dr. Nimitz every month. I don't know where she got it from, but he spent it on scholarships. That's all. It wasn't blackmail money."

"Scholarships for whom?" said Arthur. "Scholarships for Dr. Lucille Trapp."

"Who told you that?"

Arthur didn't say anything. He bit his lower lip.

"Did Dr. Erlichson tell you that he knew something about the money? Is he suggesting that Dr. Nimitz gave some of it to Dr. Trapp?"

Arthur drew back toward the door. "Dr. Erlichson's uncle told my father about it."

"Do you mean Myron Erlichson?"

"Yes, he's a banker in Grand Rapids. Very

close to my father. When my father went to Africa, Uncle Myron was the only person he kept in touch with. But someone else found out, because not long after that, the Erlichsons got an unsigned letter postmarked from Emmet, Illinois. The letter said that Uncle Myron must give Mrs. Treadwell a thousand dollars a month or else the police would be told that he had helped a criminal flee the country."

"So he gave the money to Florence," said Virginia. "He put it in her account every month, and she wrote checks on it to Dr. Nimitz for scholarships. And, yes, maybe Dr. Nimitz helped out Lucille Trapp while she was a student, even later, maybe. They're very close. That's his business." She stopped there. She didn't want to discuss Raymond Treadwell's history with Lucy Trapp—not with his son.

Arthur narrowed his eyes. "But who sent the letter to Uncle Myron in the first place? Who asked for the money? Don't you think it was the person who knew to go begging for it later—Dr. Trapp?"

She shrugged. "I'm not sure Lucy would have known about that money. More likely, it was your father himself doing the blackmail, Arthur."

"My father was in Africa by then. How could he send an anonymous letter?"

"I don't know. He managed to send a mask, didn't he?"

Arthur stepped closer. "My father sent that

mask for a reason. That mask was a message, he told me."

"A message?" She shielded her eyes to see him better against the window.

"It was my half-brother's face."

"What?"

"It was my brother Milton's face."

She put her hand down and sat there squinting, thinking. "He carved it to look like his dead son?"

"Yes."

"But—no. Nobody noticed, nobody said anything about it. Certainly, Dr. Katharde didn't notice it, and he knew your brother very well."

"My father said the mask would only look like my brother when *she* held it up to her face. That's because her eyes were his. My father said that he wanted to at least give his son his soul again, set him free. He hoped she would understand that and forgive him."

"Why didn't he just write her a letter?"

"Because he had a wife and children and saw no way of loosening himself from the chains he'd put on of his own will. But then my mother died—" Arthur paused—"and then he turned back to God, and he decided to come here to make things right. But someone did this to him! Someone did *this* to him!" The boy burst into tears.

"Arthur," said Virginia, standing up. "Who took the mask from McIlwain? Was it you?"

"Just ask the police! They won't leave me alone!"

She took a step toward him, her hand out. He turned and ran, knocking his head on a philo-dendron. She heard a door slam at the end of the house.

"Well," said Mrs. Viksma loudly, entering the room as suddenly as he'd left it (maybe she'd passed him in the hall, or then again she might have been listening). "If you've said all you need to say, Virginia, I know you probably have to get back to your business."

Virginia still had her hand out, frozen in the air. She dropped it slowly. "I didn't mean to hurt Arthur or his brothers; I never wanted to do that."

Mrs. Viksma drew herself up to her full five feet. "Well," she said dramatically, "I have no doubt that they'll be here a good while now. They have no place else to go."

"You want me to move, don't you, Mrs. Viks-ma?" No answer. Virginia walked past the land-lady to the front door. She heard silence as she closed it behind her. No insistence that she meet the Viksmas' sons sometime soon, no re-minders to be wise, careful, moral, godly. Si-lence.

She climbed back up the steps, went inside, and sat down near the telephone in her own, unfamiliar apartment. She had spent little time here in the last few days; the kitchen was clean, the refrigerator empty. Under the couch lay the binoculars she'd bought Stephen for Christmas, downtown, just a few nights ago, the very night he'd caught her staring at a sign that said, "Repent or be damned." Outside, she heard laughter, and she leaned across the bed to the window to see Mr. Viksma coming home with his two skinny sons and the two little boys. The sick one looked fine now.

The phone rang just then, such a loud ring: she ought to turn down that ringer. She went to the kitchen to get it. "Hello?"

"Ginny?"

She hesitated a second. "Merry Christmas, Mama. I was thinking about you."

"You doing all right?"

"No."

"No?"

Virginia heard her father's voice buzz like static in the background.

"I just thought I'd say Merry Christmas," said her mother, "and then, too, there's something I want to talk to you about if you have just a second—"

"What's he saying, Mama?"

More static. She heard her mother's hand over the receiver, then her muffled voice. "Well, I'm trying to tell her. Just hold on."

"What is he saying, Mama?" Virginia said angrily. Her own voice surprised her. "What is he saying about me?"

"I wanted to tell you something about church—"

"First tell me what he's saying."

"Oh, he's just saying he's concerned about

you. He wonders why you don't come home for Christmas."

"That's bull!" Virginia slammed the receiver down. How dare he mock her like that? She stood up, there in the avenue between her kitchen and her living room, put her hands over her ears, and screamed. Below her, in answer, the Viksmas' piano suddenly banged out "Silent Night, Holy Night."

She screamed again, then sobbed and struggled to catch her breath. She knew why her father mocked her that way. He had done it before, many times. He had said something kind, sweet, and then she had said something kind, sweet, and then he had burst out in an irritating laugh: *Don't get sappy on me, it makes me sick.* He liked to humiliate her; it gave him wicked pleasure. She started to pull the plug on the phone, but it rang again. She snatched it up.

"Tell him I can do without his concern—"

"Virginia?"

She stopped. "Who is this?"

"Do me a favor, would you? Be on Albert's side."

She stood up straight, startled. "Dr. Erlichson? Are you kidding?"

"Albert's not guilty, Virginia. Someone set him up."

"Excuse me, Dr. Erlichson, but I have sixteen stitches in my head to prove he's guilty. Florence knows he's guilty."

"His kid just called me—Albert's kid Arthur.

Just come with me to see him."

"I saw Arthur already."

"I mean come with me to see Albert. It's Christmas Day. I know you're not doing anything, you said you'd be alone—"

"I have a dinner invitation now, thank you very much, and I thought you were in Grand Rapids, anyway."

"What if I come over?"

"What were you doing downtown with Lucy Trapp, anyway?"

"What? When? I've talked to her several times. She's so upset about Nimitz, and she needs someone to confide in—"

She hung up the phone. She slipped Stephen's Christmas present into a grocery bag and took off through the back. No sense waiting another twenty minutes for him when she needed the walk, aching ribs or not.

It was the quietest afternoon she'd ever seen in Emmet, no traffic, no trains. A half mile away the Tower bell rang out, then the Fawcett Chapel chimes playing "God Rest Ye Merry Gentlemen," once her favorite Christmas carol, now a sermon that nagged at her, slowly, discomfortingly:

> *Remember Christ our Savior*
> *Was born on Christmas Day,*
> *To save us all from Satan's power*
> *When we had gone astray,*
> *O tidings of comfort and joy.*

She stopped, suddenly. "Albert Amalya couldn't have put those keys in my purse," she said firmly, declaring it to the clear street. "So who did?"

She began walking again, more briskly. She slid as she stepped off asphalt onto sidewalk, and put her hand against a thin, forking birch to steady herself. Dr. Nimitz? Was he a blackmailer? Had he conspired with Albert in Florence's kidnapping just in order to help frame Amalya later? After all, Dr. Nimitz loved Lucy Trapp; maybe he wanted revenge for whatever Amalya had done to her years ago. Dr. Nimitz ought to have recognized Amalya on stage with him in the Christmas pageant: "I saw Edward look at me from the stage," Amalya had said, whether that was true or not—yet Dr. Nimitz never even mentioned it. Virginia imagined Dr. Nimitz heading up to the office on Wednesday night with Florence's keys (attic and Tower keys!) in his hand. She imagined Amalya whispering to him at the pageant, "Get these back in her purse." She imagined Dr. Nimitz walking nervously up to an office he thought was empty, dropping the keys in the only purse on Florence's desk, not realizing it belonged to Virginia.

Adrenaline charged through her now, the adrenaline of honesty. Besides Dr. Nimitz, Dr. Trapp, and Dr. Katharde, only she and Stephen had been in the building the night of the party. Dr. Molliby hadn't received an invitation, or so he said, and Dr. Erlichson had been locked out for most of the evening, or so he said—but he could have found an opportunity to slip upstairs and put Florence's keys in what he thought was Florence's purse. One of them had done it, but which one?

She rang the doorbell but turned the knob and pushed the door open. In the middle of the entryway, Stephen stood in an apron, his eyes closed, beating time to the "Hallelujah" chorus with a gravy ladle. The music swelled to its last, rich chord and stopped, leaving a ring in the empty air.

"Merry Christmas," she said.

"What?" He opened the plastic bag and looked at the unwrapped box. "Binoculars! And so festively packaged. Your present's under the tree—want it?"

"Not now. Take off that apron, Stephen. We have to go back to McIlwain."

17

R.F.

VIRGINIA SWITCHED ON HER DESK LAMP, casting pale light over the ruins of the office. She steadied her swivel chair and drew open a desk drawer with a slow, heavy rumble. "Florence keeps carbons in her filing cabinet. Looks like the police put the files back. We'll each take a drawer."

Stephen wiped a question mark of gravy off his collar. "And just what am I looking for, again?"

"Letters between Raymond Treadwell and Florence. She said she destroyed them all, but I know Florence. She's pretty scatterbrained. She might have left something lying around, even an envelope, something to show she'd been in contact with him. I want to know if anyone around the department could have found out about Treadwell."

"How about old computer files—does she have a PC?"

"Welcome to the Dark Ages." Virginia handed him a stack of folders, then rolled her chair back to her own desk and started to read.

"You sure it's O.K. to be doing this?" he said.

She didn't answer, but frowned and pulled out a group of folders filed in the second drawer under *T*.

> Teleology Temptation Thomas, Doubting Transcendent Being Transfiguration Turpitude, Moral

"Florence has her correspondence filed topically," Virginia said, "instead of by name. Where would she file a letter to Treadwell, a.k.a. Amalya?"

"Husbands, Ex."

"I doubt it, Stephen."

"I don't see any rhyme or reason to the letters in this file," he said. "Look here. In the middle of a bunch of Katharde's letters to some paleontologist in London, I find a carbon of a note to Florence's doctor."

"Look, Stephen, this is weird."

"What?"

"There are some letters pulled out. I remember Florence mentioning this correspondent on our last morning here. Listen.

"December 11

Dear Mrs. Treadwell,

I'm afraid I have to put an end to this correspondence. I am empty and anxious. I
sense only darkness in the universe. Wherever light shines, darkness swallows it up.

R.F."

"You must have read the last letter in the series,"
said Stephen. "The guy sounds pretty bad off."
"Here's another." She flipped backwards in
the pile and read,

"November 21

Dear Mrs. Treadwell,

So, we are still corresponding. I thought by
now that Milton would have written to me
himself. I guess no mere apologist can
match the zeal of a secretary when it comes
to feeling the pain of a fellow human being.
You say that you have been in darkness and
know that God is there. I was once as zeal-
ous as you; I had faith as great as yours,
but deep despair overwhelmed me, and
God was not. 'Not what?' you ask? He *was*
not. I fell and I did not meet his hands; I
took the leap of faith and my foot never

touched solid earth. He was not. Perhaps, for you, he is. Or perhaps your pit has not yet been as deep as mine.

R.F."

"So how does Florence respond to that?" Stephen asked.

"Her responses aren't here. They must be filed somewhere else."

"Read another from R.F.," Stephen said. "Read the first in the pile."

"Oh, come on, I've seen enough. This has nothing to do with Raymond Treadwell."

"Let's find out what his problem is."

"I know exactly what his problem is." She looked up and tossed the folder to Stephen. "The guy is a whiny atheist—"

Stephen smiled. "Like you?"

"I'm not whiny. Anyway, Florence is taking it upon herself to write back because MPK is too busy, and now the guy's upset."

Stephen reached over and pulled the loose letters out of the folder, thumbed through them, dropped a few out, and picked one up from the floor.

"September 5

Dear Mrs. Treadwell,

Thank you very much for taking the time

to supply me with a copy of pp. 76–77 of vol. 3 of the *Christian Scholar's Encyclopedia.* However, leave the religious counsel to Milton; it doesn't become you. I devoted my life to the service of God, but He passed me over unjustly. Like Cain, like Esau, like Saul, I could not please God. He created me but did not love me. He preferred liars and prodigals. He lifted up the wicked and passed over the righteous. When the wicked returned to the shores of the righteous, He forgave them and restored them. He restored their children and gave them new offspring. But the righteous He forgot. He sent them to slavery and the grave, took away the wives of their youth, and gave them no fruit. Their names died with them. I am a righteous man, and I have been passed over. My only revenge on God is unbelief.

To serve God is to wear a mask made by another, to smile at the cruelty of holiness when the heart shrinks in terror. I prefer to stand naked in my terror and serve the one who will not abandon me in the grave, because the grave belongs to him. I therefore declare my former religion a lie. There is no justice in dreams. I announce my freedom from dreams, from a God who would sift out the righteous and save the chaff. I shall have no resurrection.

Rafiel Fawcett"

The Tower, the Mask, and the Grave

Stephen looked at Virginia. She licked her lips, as she'd seen Goodman do. "Rafiel Fawcett?" she said. "The name sounds so much like Rafis Johansen Fawcett."

"Rafis Fawcett," Stephen mumbled. "Rafiel Fawcett. You think it could be a descendant?"

"What's the address on those letters?" she asked.

"Just a Chicago P.O. box."

She scooted her chair close to him and looked for a long time at the carbon. "Interesting."

"Yeah. That part about the mask—"

"Save those. I want to ask Florence about them."

He folded the letters up and tucked them in his coat pocket. Virginia started back to her own drawer, but suddenly Stephen laughed out loud.

"What now?"

"Look at this, Virginia. Look—hah!" He laughed so loudly that she jumped up and shut the door. "Sorry, Ginny. There's this letter stuck in here, wrong file again; it's to the board of the—let's see—Institute for Intellectual Evangelism."

"What's the date on that?"

"December 16."

"Oh yeah. Florence typed that on that our last day at work. I remember Dr. Katharde asking about it."

"Hey, listen to this:

Dear Chairman,

It would indeed give me great pleasure to address the annual conference of the IIE. I am more convinced than ever that our association is vital to the defense of God's kingdom. I look forward to seeing you all in February, and I plan to bring my secretary with me, as I desperately need all the hell she can give me in preparing my lectures.

Milton Katharde"

Virginia squinted. "All the what?"

"Hah!" Stephen roared. *"Help,* he means. *Help!* Wow, what a goof."

"Wonder if it went out that way," Virginia said. "Florence usually catches her mistakes."

"Probably Katharde caught the typo when he signed it."

"No, no, Florence typed it that last Friday before vacation and signed it herself with his stamp. She had to leave early that day. She told him to look at the copy, but the original was already in the mail."

"And when did the mail go out?" Stephen frowned and stuck out his lips. "Not till late afternoon, most likely, since it was a holiday, and they're always short-handed at the college post office on holidays. Katharde could have fished the letter out of the office mailbox if he really wanted to. He could have typed it over."

"Him? Type a letter?" Virginia snickered. "I'm sure he wouldn't have gone any further than correcting the old one. I'll look at the correction ribbon, see if anyone typed an *l* at the end of the day." She leaned down near the typewriter.

"Surely he'd have used whiteout, Virginia. It's a lot easier."

"He doesn't like that stuff. Anyway, it's easy to roll a letter back into this old machine to make a correction. Florence does it all the time." She reached into the silvery stomach of the typewriter and pulled out the new ribbon. It unraveled immediately in her lap, then dropped on the floor and rolled toward Stephen.

"There's nothing on this ribbon," Stephen said. "It's brand-new. Hey, no, I'm wrong. There is one letter. An *l!*" He smiled up, obviously self-satisfied. "I was right. Katharde, or somebody, did change it."

"I remember Florence said she was almost out of ribbon that day. Dr. Katharde must have put a new one on."

"Virginia, did Florence say she typed a letter to Amalya that afternoon at work?"

Virginia nodded.

"I wonder," he said, "if she made any corrections on that letter."

Virginia looked at the pile of white tape still curled up at Stephen's feet. "What are you saying? That someone could have read some of

Florence's letter to Treadwell off a used-up correction ribbon?"

"What do you think? Seems possible."

"I think it's unlikely. Florence doesn't usually make that many mistakes. Even if she corrected his name, for instance, and someone happened to read it off the ribbon—well, she told me she mailed the invitations to the party from home. It's not like anyone could have gone looking for the whole letter at her house and found out about what she was planning for Wednesday night."

"Wonder what happened to the old correction ribbon," said Stephen.

Virginia opened Florence's top drawer, thinking. Florence *had* mentioned that she was making a lot of mistakes that day. There was no correction ribbon in here. Not in the other drawers, either. She must have thrown it away.

"Why don't I go downstairs and make another copy of this letter?" said Stephen. "We can show it to Deacon and see what he thinks."

"All right," said Virginia slowly. "I'll keep looking around. Seems like there must be a letter to Raymond Treadwell here somewhere." She placed the files she had removed back into the drawer, then she went to the window and looked out over campus. She had looked out on the campus the night Florence disappeared. She had seen the two little boys—Albert Amalya's sons, probably—playing on the sidewalk, and then a pair of men walking away with them.

One must have been Albert himself. Raymond Treadwell.

She felt a breeze from her left. Something glittered in the corner of her eye, and she turned to see the glass roses above Dr. Katharde's door tremble blue at the edges as the door wafted open slightly. Deacon must have left it unlocked. Virginia started to close it but changed her mind and pushed it open. The door fell back, silently, and bumped the closet behind it. The great octagonal table lay turned over on its side, pinned against a bookshelf. A long pair of feet in black slippers splayed from behind it.

"Dr. Katharde?" said Virginia, rushing in. "Dr. Katharde, is that you?" She pulled the table up and dropped to the floor with a yelp. He lay white as a sheet on a blood-red circle of carpet, struggling for breath. Next to him lay a gun. She reached immediately for the phone, but he lifted his arm and grabbed her ankle weakly.

"No," he said.

"I'm calling an ambulance."

"I want to tell you something," he rasped. "Come closer, I don't know how long I have."

She clenched her teeth and took her hand away from the phone, from help. She bent down obediently, glancing at him up and down, trying to make out where he'd been shot.

"Raymond has murdered me," he said. "He shot me in the back. He who hates his brother has murdered in his heart. A murderer shall not enter the kingdom of heaven!" He tried to shout it, but his voice wouldn't carry above a gurgle. She stood up and lifted the phone, shaking.

"Treadwell's in prison," she said.

"No, he's escaped again."

She sat back slightly on her haunches. "No—that's *impossible,* Dr. Katharde."

"He brought me here and left me. He wants to kill me. He wants to kill Florence, too. He's the child of the father of lies."

"911," she mumbled, "911," as if it were the Lord's Prayer. She got to her feet and punched the buttons on the telephone. Busy! She dialed again, got the same signal, and looked at the old man stretched out on the floor. She knew she ought to look for the wound herself, try to staunch the blood, but just the thought made her see stars. "Listen, I'll be right back, Dr. Katharde. I have to get some help." She put the receiver by his ear (Why? What sense did that make?) and ran out of the office, down the hall, down the west stairs, to find Stephen.

"Stephen?" she called as she ran to the door of the copy office on the first floor. "Stephen?" The outer office was dark, the door to the inner copy room locked. She checked the basement copy room on the west side, then flew back up the basement steps. He must have headed up to the department again from another direction, or she would have run into him.

She ran to the east side of the building,

breathing hard, and took three steps at a time up to the third floor. As she hurried down the hall to the central stairs, she glanced at the artifacts case, fifteen feet away, crouching in its dim corner without its glass.

"Stephen?" Virginia shouted. "Stephen, are you around here?"

She heard a creak on the floor above her and ran for the steps again. This time, as she passed Walford Lecture Hall, she held her hand out in front of her in case the door opened and the man in the hood came out again. The man in the black hood. Raymond Treadwell. In jail, no matter what Dr. Katharde said.

"Stephen? Stephen?" She bounded up the central steps and down the hall to the department. Stephen stepped out of the office door.

"What's the matter?" he said.

"Take a look in Dr. Katharde's office and you'll see—he's hurt!"

Stephen went in and called out, "Nobody's here!" just as she came around the corner into the department. She looked into Dr. Katharde's office. It was empty. The circle of blood still marked his spot on the floor, but the octagonal table was upended. The receiver of the telephone rested in its cradle. "Just a minute ago, he was here. Really, Stephen, you see the blood. He told me Treadwell had shot him in the back."

"He told you *Treadwell* had shot him? He's flipped."

"He's probably trying to climb downstairs on

his own," said Virginia. "He's in no shape to walk."

Stephen stood quietly for a second. "I'll go after him, Ginny. He probably took the east steps, since I came up the west."

"I could have missed him, too. I took the central stairs."

"You stay right here. Back in a minute." Stephen headed quickly out the door.

Virginia stood by the window and stared down in case Dr. Katharde left the building by one of the north doors.

Finally she went into the hall, thinking how little she liked to be up here by herself. She drifted toward the east wing after Stephen—maybe she ought to have done what he said and stayed put—but soon she was past the central stairs and into the seminar room that overlooked the Shade Hall lawn. She stopped and stared anxiously at the snow, the Christmas lights, the blue sky, then went out into the fifth-floor hall again. The attic door, to her right, stood wide open. Had Deacon left it that way?

She stepped inside. Someone had left the drawstring light on. It felt cold in here today, colder than usual. Now that the police were gone the heat was off again. The romantic chatter on the walls looked threatening, dancing jaggedly around her shadow, skipping behind the wires of the big cages.

"Dr. Katharde?" she said weakly. Could he have come up here? Probably not. She began searching for him the way you search for lost keys, looking everywhere, even places you knew they couldn't be.

She would have—could have—stopped at the end of the second long room, but before her lay the third attic, and then the chamber below the bell, and in that direction, strangely enough, black as it was here so far from the light, she thought she could faintly make out the frame of that chamber door.

She walked closer, bouncing gently along the bridge, squinting. She saw the entrance to the tunnel faintly as she passed.

"Dr. Katharde? Are you up here?" She walked over two more bridges, then reached out her hands and crossed the threshold of the bell chamber. As she entered, she realized where the light came from. It came from above. The Tower door stood open at the top of the ladder.

She put one foot on a rung and stopped. "Dr. Katharde?"

This time she had shouted. Why didn't he answer?

Her legs moved underneath her. They carried her into the cold, the blue of the world. The wind slapped her as she emerged from the Tower, and she squinted against the brilliant sky.

Dr. Katharde stood beside the bell in his long black bathrobe, wearing the mask.

"What are you doing?" she said. "Come down."

He clenched his fists. The mask leered.

"Come on," she said. She stepped out into the

Tower. "You're hurt. I need to take you to a hospital.

"Do you know who I am?" he said. His voice was rough, low. He held both hands to his side, and blood oozed over his fingers.

"Of course I do."

"I am perfection. I have won Satan over to my side."

"What?"

"Do you believe that I have won Satan over to my side?" he said.

"Dr. Katharde, I don't even believe in Satan."

The mask was still for a moment. The carved face look uncertain, but then a cold wind of resolution blew around the Tower and escaped into the sky.

He moved a step closer to her. When he breathed it sounded like a rubber duck being squeezed in, out. She imagined blood pumping from his side with each breath. "Years ago," he whispered, "my friend turned his back on us. He offended his students, chased wanton women, deserted his wife, forced himself on Lucille Trapp, and then tried to kill us all. But I forgave him, thinking God would take vengeance. I prayed for him. I waited. For twenty years I supported his deserted wife and his forsaken children."

"You were the blackmailer, weren't you?" said Virginia, gasping against the wind. "You didn't support her, you blackmailed Myron Erlichson to do it."

"I was the benefactor. When Myron told me he was supposed to pay Florence's support each month, I asked him to transfer the money from the accounts I kept at his bank: royalty money that I seldom use."

"But who told Myron Erlichson to pay the money in the first place? Who blackmailed him?"

"It's my business how I did it!" He pitched forward suddenly, grabbing her wrist to keep from falling into the trap door.

"Dr. Katharde—"

"I was like Cain, like Saul. I had done right, but I had no reward. No one to carry on my kingdom. And Treadwell had not only his daughters but also three sons. He ought to have suffered for abandoning his family, but God blessed him."

"How could you be so jealous, Dr. Katharde? He'd lost everything."

Dr. Katharde stood back against a pillar of the Tower. He wrapped his arms around it. "I didn't know how I hated him, until he returned. When I saw his children—"

"How did you know he'd come back?"

"I saw him cleaning in the building late one evening. He was changed, but I saw him scrubbing a wall, and he turned his face from me. I pretended not to know him. I knew that he would try to see Florence again. She would take him back. All would be forgiven. I found the letter she wrote to him, inviting him here."

"How did you find it?" asked Virginia. "She mailed it from home, with the party invitations."

Dr. Katharde didn't answer. The mask turned toward the campus lawn. "Look there," he said. "Look at the sign there."

"'Let the Kingdom Stand,'" Virginia read.

"The kingdom does stand, Miss Falls. No one can conquer God. Neither by arguing with him, nor by defending him. I have travailed here for over forty years to give birth to a great faith, and I have fallen short. My life has been nothing but filthy rags. Heaven's door is closed to me. Only the doors of hell lie open wide."

"Aren't you afraid of hell?" Virginia shivered in the strong cold.

The mask turned left, right. "I'm not afraid of Satan. God rewards the wicked, those who sin and repent, but Satan rewards those who have no need of repentance."

"Blackmail, kidnapping—don't those call for repentance? Does Satan reward those deeds?" She strained to see his eyes. She couldn't see them for the shadows.

"I thought you didn't believe in Satan," he said.

"Dr. Katharde, you kidnapped Florence."

"No."

"You did."

He was silent for a moment. Then, with all his breath he shrieked through the mouth of the mask, "I didn't!"

"You saw the correction ribbon, didn't you?

273

You realized she had written a letter to him, so you went to her house and took the letters from the mailbox."

Silence. Grass whipped around the edge of the mask. It fell back from his forehead, and she saw two words clearly: *No Resurrection.* Virginia felt the sky drop across her shoulders. "You're R.F.," she said. "You're Rafiel Fawcett. You must have known about Rafis Fawcett, you must have read about the tunnel in her memoirs. Dr. Katharde, why would you put Florence in that hole? How could you do it?"

"She would have taken him back!" Dr. Katharde leaned back into the wire around the Tower. He pulled back the leering mask to breathe easier, but his own pale face was horrible, stiff with pain, obscenely angry. "She had to know how low he really is, how *wicked* and *faithless* he really is. I had to show her what he's capable of!"

"But you're the one who hurt her—you're the wicked one!"

"No, I've taken *care* of her!" He lifted the wire and put one bony leg underneath. "I'd have given my life to save her from him! I would do it even now—"

Virginia started toward him. "What are you doing?"

He dropped something into the trap door of the attic and then hoisted his other leg over with a terrible grunt. She lunged and grabbed him by the arm, but he had already slipped from the

Tower to the rooftop, raking the ice with his fingernails as he fell.

Virginia screamed. She saw his eyes open wide, his mouth form a wet circle, and then he vanished.

Epilogue

"WHAT IS THE ULTIMATE REASON FOR all this suffering?" said Dr. Molliby. He was the first who dared to speak after the funeral. Virginia sat between him and Stephen on the fountain near Fawcett Chapel, looking across the gray mush of campus to McIlwain Hall. The others sat or stood nearby: Dr. Erlichson and his wife, Dr. Nimitz, Dr. Trapp, each facing a different direction, each silent.

"Do you really believe that there's a structure to our lives?" said Virginia. "A pattern?"

Dr. Molliby nodded. "Oh my, yes." Wisps of his goatee blew up over his jaw.

"I see no pattern," she said. "It's like that card game, where someone throws the deck up in the air and they land in no order at all."

"Fifty-two pickup," said Dr. Erlichson.

"The difficulty in that idea," said Dr. Molliby, "is that even in a seemingly random game, there are predictable results. One only lacks the information to make accurate predictions."

"So our difficulty here on earth is just a lack of information," said Virginia.

"Yes."

"Surely there's a greater difficulty to be faced," mumbled Dr. Nimitz.

"What is that, Edward?" Dr. Molliby snapped. "What greater difficulty must we now face? Tell us."

"The greater difficulty," Dr. Nimitz said in his high, cottony voice, "lies not in accepting that structure and meaning exist in the world but in believing that the elements of the structure matter as much as the whole. That every person's life is not only a pathway but also the end of a journey."

"Edward!" sputtered Dr. Molliby. "You know I've always believed that the stone is as vital as the pyramid. Anyone created in *imago dei* has his own *telos.*"

"I'm sorry, dear Howard. I didn't mean that as an attack on your ideas—"

"Oh, you two and your unfettered ideas!" moaned Dr. Trapp, standing a few feet away. She clutched her black wool cap and veil to her head. "Milton's dead. Raymond Treadwell's back. There, I've put it in real language. Call it what it is; say what you mean."

"We were trying, darling," Dr. Nimitz said

weakly. Dr. Molliby raised his eyebrows and sniffed in silent reprisal. A sudden wind startled them. It was a raging cold wind, bringing January on its back. The wave surged through dry trees, through sticks and grass. It surged through teeth and hair and bones. Virginia and Dr. Molliby bent into the collars of their coats, but the others had to turn their backs to it, so they all ended up in the same direction. When they lifted their heads, they saw Detective Deacon making his way over from Fawcett Chapel in a black suit.

"Hello," called out Dr. Erlichson to the detective. "We're all taking advantage of this fine funeral weather to discuss the even finer points of teleology. Why don't you join us?"

"Good afternoon," Deacon said. "Nice funeral."

"Oh yes," said Dr. Erlichson, "that's what we've all been saying. It was a *nice* funeral."

Deacon cleared his throat. "The guy must have known everybody from here to eternity."

"Yes, he knew us," said Dr. Trapp without looking up. "And we knew him—at least we knew that he was brilliant, that he was kind and generous, and that he would have sacrificed practically anything for our happiness. Those are the things we'll remember." She rocked forwards and took a step toward the chapel, holding her hat on. "I've got to go. Goodbye, everyone."

"Lucy—," said Dr. Nimitz. "Wait."

"Don't follow me, Edward. I want to be alone."

"I say something wrong?" asked Deacon to the others. He shrugged and turned to go. Virginia walked after Dr. Trapp. She wanted to comfort her, but she wasn't sure how. She wasn't entirely sure that she'd keep following rather than turn away toward the library once they crossed the road.

"Lucy!" someone called as Virginia stepped onto the opposite curb. "Lucy!" Virginia looked up quickly, in time to avoid bumping into Raymond Treadwell, who was clean-shaven and dressed in a dark suit and bolo tie. Florence stood next to him, and they both faced Dr. Trapp, who cringed a few feet away next to the skinny pole of a No Parking sign. The Treadwells together looked like an old photograph of some immigrant couple just off the boat: stiffly dressed but haggard, eager but sad.

Virginia hurried past them, embarrassed, hoping they hadn't noticed her. Stephen waited for her a few feet away. "Want to go downtown for coffee?" he asked and took her hand in his. She found comfort in the familiarity of this, in his persistence and her own primness. Both of them wore thick gloves, but there was comfort even in the small warmth that passed between them. And so they began walking. As they reached downtown Emmet, a long gray car pulled up beside them and stopped. The driver's window made a purring sound as it sank down. Goodman looked out.

"Can we get coffee somewhere?" he said.

"Sure," said Stephen. "Your treat."

Goodman rolled his window up again and pulled the car into a nearby space at Anita's Pancake Palace. A few moments later all three sat in a booth under smiling Anita. A waitress brought them coffee, and Stephen thanked her cheerfully. He ordered chocolate chip pancakes, stirred three teaspoonfuls of sugar into his coffee, and reached for the cream.

"I wanted to show you two this," said Goodman. He pulled a white disk from his pocket. "Deacon found it up in the Tower. It's a typewriter correction ribbon."

Stephen took it and pulled the ribbon out, holding it up to the light for her to see:

yaR tseraedD

"Dearest Ray," he read, turning it over and around.

"Did Florence type this?" asked Virginia.

Goodman nodded. "She put an extra *d* on *Dearest,* so in order to correct it, she held down the correction button and backed up all the way to the beginning of the word."

"You say you found it in the Tower?"

"Yes."

"Then that's what Dr. Katharde threw back in the bell chamber. I wondered what it was."

Goodman put the ribbon back in his pocket. "It was his form of a confession."

Virginia remembered the moment, the mask, the cry. "I guess when he saw this," she said, "he knew Florence had written a letter to Raymond Treadwell. Katharde couldn't find it in the office mail, so he went to her house and looted her mailbox."

"Along with the letter, he found the party invitations," said Goodman. "He figured out that Mrs. Treadwell was planning a sort of Christmas/surprise/welcome-home party for her husband, and he was horrified. He thought the best thing to do was mail all the letters and find a way to turn everyone against Treadwell for good. Make him out to be a deranged kidnapper."

"That would do it," said Stephen.

"At his house we found rough drafts of the letters he'd sent her from R.F. We don't know when he found out about the tunnel or how he linked it with Rafis Fawcett: most likely he'd read her journals in the archives. Anyway, he probably knew about the entrance in the Tower well before last Wednesday. Mrs. Treadwell says he borrowed her keys a couple of times last month. Maybe that's when he located it."

Goodman turned sideways in the booth and stretched one leg out. Virginia had never seen him so relaxed. "So," he said, "sometime after he found out about Mrs. Treadwell's plan to meet her husband, he came up with this idea of staging a kidnapping, putting her down in the tunnel, and pinning the blame on Treadwell. We don't know why he held out Molliby's invitation to the party. Maybe he intended to mail it but accidentally left it behind, or maybe he knew he'd have attic insulation on his clothes that night and he was afraid Molliby would start sneezing all over the place—give him away."

"What I don't understand," said Stephen, "is how he could have done it—I mean, how did he actually do it? He was in a Christmas pageant the night she was kidnapped, right? And we established that it had to have happened between 7:30 and 8:30, the exact hours of the show."

"But there was a tunnel entrance in Fawcett Chapel," said Virginia.

"Still. Don't tell me there was time between costume changes to climb through a tunnel to McIlwain and kidnap a woman."

"No," said Goodman. "There wasn't. We think he went up to the department before the pageant and waited for Mrs. Treadwell—probably in his own office, which explains why it was unlocked. Thing was, she found that mask hanging on the tree and felt she had to put it back in the case. He followed her to the third floor, hit her over the head with a hammer he'd brought along for shoring up beams in the tunnel. He smashed the case in the process. Dropped his hammer, too. He took her up to the Tower using her keys and then carried her down to the tunnel. After he tied her up, he went over to Fawcett Chapel and came out in the men's-room closet. Later he returned Mrs. Treadwell's keys to Miss Falls's purse—by accident!"

"Then I threw them to Mark Erlichson," said Virginia. "That made him look kind of suspicious. I mean, I kept wondering why he was in the building the night we decorated. There were these odd things about him."

"Nothing so odd about him." said Goodman. "His wife kicked him out of the house Monday night while she gave a Mary Kay party. He came over to McIlwain to play video games in the computer lab—guess he left his office light on."

"What *did* happen to Florence's key to the building?"

"She'd mailed it to Treadwell so that he could get in the building that night. She says she had an extra in a compartment of her purse, that's how she let herself in."

"And where was her purse?"

"We never found it. When Katharde realized he'd put the keys in *your* purse, Miss Falls, he must have found hers and gotten rid of it. I believe Katharde's original plan was to pretend to stumble on Treadwell, alert the police, and then help them find Mrs. Treadwell in the tunnel. Problem was, Miss Falls stumbled on Treadwell first. That threw everything off. Katharde doubled back to the attic to finish nailing the boards in place over the tunnel entrance—since he'd dropped his hammer he grabbed a hardback volume of Shakespeare from the English department—but it turned out that's exactly where Treadwell was hiding. Treadwell heard him coming and escaped over the roof, down the west side, using the belt of his pageant costume as a rope to lower himself onto the fire escape."

"Then Dr. Katharde never really watched from a fifth-floor window," said Virginia. "He lied about that."

"No surprise there," said Stephen.

She shrugged her shoulders. "I know it sounds crazy, but it still surprises me that he'd lie like that. What about the mask? Who stole it from McIlwain?"

"Arthur Amalya, just like we thought. He knew it was important to his father and that somebody was after it. He went over to McIlwain in one of his father's custodial uniforms and lifted the mask—took it home for safekeeping." Goodman brought his long leg back and sat up. He seemed too large for the booth.

"So Arthur took the mask, but Katharde left the ransom note?" asked Stephen.

"Exactly," said Goodman.

"And how did Katharde get the mask back?"

"He knew from Mrs. Treadwell's letter to her husband that Raymond Treadwell had three sons with the last name *Amalya*. He called your landlords and pretended to be a friend in order to find out Arthur's address downtown. Then he went into Chicago on Friday evening, broke into the apartment, searched for the mask, and found it. He was supposed to pick up Molliby that same evening for a church service, and when he finally came late, Molliby says, he came from the wrong direction, from the city side. The two of them never made it to church, either. They ran into the two of you, picked you up, and then followed us when we chased down Treadwell."

"The guy I wrestled in the Tower was no kid," said Stephen. "It wasn't Arthur."

"No, the angel of death touched you, Mr. Holc. Katharde wrestled you."

"Katharde? You're kidding. An old man like that gave me a concussion?"

Goodman looked amused. "Maybe you should take up weightlifting, Mr. Holc. He came up that afternoon to leave us a clue as to Mrs. Treadwell's whereabouts. He didn't want to hurt her, after all; he just wanted to get Treadwell in trouble. He'd probably already left some boards out of place over the tunnel entrance, but we didn't notice it, so that next afternoon he repaired the wall and left us a message: No Resurrection." Goodman smiled and shook his head. He held up the correction ribbon. "In the end, Katharde told the truth by leaving us this last bit of information. I guess he thought he was doing right all along, saving the world from Raymond Treadwell."

"That's what happens," said Stephen almost cheerfully, "when a man tries to play God."

"All his worst qualities bubble up to the surface," said Goodman. "Anger, bitterness, jealousy, envy. The more noble a man's ambition, the higher his goal, the uglier the road that leads him there."

"Amen."

Virginia sighed, feeling unusually out of place, watching Stephen once again accept his great plate of pancakes. "What are you going to do?" she asked Goodman.

"Oh, I'm only having coffee."

"I mean, now that this mess is finished. I guess you'll go back where you came from. Where is that?"

He sipped from his cup. "Chicago. All over. I visit a lot of places, I meet a lot of people."

"Sounds like a life Virginia would enjoy," said Stephen, raising his eyebrows. "Maybe you two should get together."

"How about you two?" said Goodman. He looked back and forth between them. "You got any plans?"

Stephen coughed and sipped his coffee. "Guess I'll keep working on that master's, teaching piano, et cetera. How about you, Ginny? 'I know it's late, I know you're weary, I know your plans, they don't include me, but still here we are—' "

"Hush." She sat back against the hard cushion of the booth and tried to pull her unruly hair into a ponytail. "I can't see committing myself to anything for now. I need a job, obviously. Guess I'll start looking."

"Try the FBI." Goodman smiled. "And how about the Tower?" His brown eyes were the same color as Anita's on the wall. It was his independence that was attractive, Virginia thought. His I'll-be-going-now-see-you-never-againness.

"What do you mean 'how about the Tower?'" she asked.

"You two going up there again? Maybe to ring that bell?"

Virginia shook her head. "I never want to see that Tower again."

Stephen smiled. "Love is kind of a leap of faith," he said. "Ginny likes to have her feet on the ground at all times."

"Really?" asked Goodman with a mischievous smile. "The girl who fell a hundred feet in the dark, broke nine or ten ribs, rolled down a staircase, and then chased a man out of a tunnel and overpowered him—"

"He turned out to be innocent," she added.

"This girl is afraid of commitment?"

"I'm not afraid of anything," she said defensively. "I know what I want, that's all. When I find the man I want, he won't follow me around waiting on me. He won't apologize all the time. He'll expect me to do the pleasing, and if I don't he won't stick around whining on and on about it."

Stephen looked at her and bit his lower lip. The skin went white around his teeth.

"Maybe you need to take the bull by the horns, so to speak," Goodman said to Stephen. "Sounds like she wants a man who'll stand up for himself."

"I do stand up for himself," he said firmly

and looked hard at Virginia. "But if she wants someone to treat her badly, she'll have to look elsewhere. I happen to love her too much."

Virginia rolled her eyes. Goodman handed her a paper bag containing her bloodstained tennis shoes, which she planned to throw away as soon as she got home. He gulped down his coffee, said a short goodbye, and left. Outside, she saw the burial procession on its way out of town. She had chosen not to go to the burial site, but watching the long black car pass by, she imagined for a second that she was crossing out giant exclamation points, replacing them with ellipses and double hyphens, replacing certainty with uncertainty. Sometimes life looked like a descent into darkness, a vanishing wail. No purpose to it at all.

"Sure you don't want some pancakes?" asked Stephen.

"Oh, why not?" she said. "Give me eight or ten."

Late that afternoon, after long hours of walking alone on the railroad path, she lay on her couch to read a magazine. She put on a recording of Stephen playing the *Goldberg Variations*—he even hummed along, like Glenn Gould—and chastised herself for insulting him earlier. What kind of man *did* she want, anyway? She stretched her legs under a blanket. Miranda curled up by her shoulder, tickling her ear with a loud purr. Someone knocked.

"Stephen?" she shouted. "Did you come for an apology?"

"No," a man's voice shouted back, "UPS."

She winced, then stood and opened the door and took a package out of the man's raw hands. A large box, maybe two feet by three feet. He ran back down the stairs, and she went into the kitchen to fish a knife out of a kitchen drawer. She dispatched the packing tape quickly enough. Balled-up newspapers popped out of the box before she'd pulled it open. *The Tallahassee Times.*

She opened up the card attached to the square red package inside the cardboard flaps.

Dear Ginny,

Want you to know the good news before anyone else. Recently, as I tried to tell you on the phone yesterday, I have attended church every Sunday. The pastor has visited our home to talk to me about my heavenly hope, which I am ashamed to say I did not have. Your father said a few things, which I didn't think he shouldof, and went out to have a smoke. But that preacher really did get me thinking. I remembered the light you had in you as a child, your face always shining so bright that you were more like an angel child than my own. I want that, too, so, on Christmas Day (near to the time you read this), I will be baptized and give my testimony. I have so much more to tell you and to ask you about the Bible, since you know so much more than I do about it even at your young age. But mainly I want to say that I love you with all my heart, and if you cannot come to Florida this winter, perhaps your father will take me on a trip to Illinois in the spring. I have never seen your apartment or even your college for that matter, and I have missed you so much. Have a happy Christmas, do not be alone, take care of yourself, and eat right.

In Jesus' Love,
Your Mama

P.S. Pray for your daddy's salvation.

Virginia unwrapped the package, her hands shaking, and pulled out a coat her mother had bought for her. It was red, with tiny tiny pictures of palm trees woven in across the shoulders. Putting the coat on was almost like feeling her mother's arms around her neck. It was warm— not the kind of thing you could buy in Florida, more likely purchased from a catalog. She sat for a moment looking at it and then couldn't endure to sit anymore—or stand, or walk, or anything else that involved legs. She picked up the phone to call Stephen.

"Hello?" he said.

"Hi, Stephen. First of all, I'm sorry for what I said." She cleared her throat and let out a long breath—still not ready to let go, maybe never ready to fall, and on the other hand possibly a tiny step closer to dropping right over the edge—she hadn't forgotten, after all, the two wonderful minutes on the floor, though that seemed like a long time ago now. "Hey, can you come over? I got this letter from my mother, and I feel—well, I can't describe how I feel. I can read it to you while you make us supper and give me my Christmas present. What is my present, anyway?"

He gave a sly laugh. "That, my dear Virginia, will have to remain a mystery."